Based

Mike Stone

Ye that love the LORD hate evil.

Psalm 97

Chapter 1

Ryan Turner was standing alone on the subway platform when he saw the punch coming. It was only a blur out of the corner of his eye, but he recognized it immediately and ducked his head. The punch clipped his shoulder. His assailant, a black male in his late teens, backed up, eyes wild and confused. He wasn't expecting a fight.

Ryan took two quick steps and slammed a straight right fist into the teen's jaw. It landed with a sharp crack that echoed across the underground platform. The youth staggered back and fell full length and lay still. His jaw, most likely broken, already starting to swell.

Ryan stood stunned. The exchange had lasted only seconds, but he panted for air and his heart thumped wildly against his chest.

Another boy appeared at his side, eyes wide with excitement, and said, "Dude, are you okay?"

Ryan gave the boy a quick look and scanned the area. It was five-thirty in the morning and they were the only ones on the subway platform at Hollywood and Vine. "Yeah, man," he said.

A horn blared. A blast of wind erupted from the subway tunnel. Ryan and the boy stared down at the black teen lying unconscious at their feet. The gust from the tunnel ruffled their hair and clothes.

"Do you know that guy?" the boy asked.

Ryan shook his head. "Never saw him before in my life." The wind took the words from his mouth and blew them away. He spoke louder. "It's called the Knockout Game. They sneak up on a white person and sucker punch 'em when they're not looking. It's usually a woman or an old person who gets hit." He nodded down at the black teen. "He must have thought I was an easy mark, standing here by myself, daydreaming."

"I guess he found out the hard way you weren't."

"Yeah, right."

Wind swept over the platform. It flattened their clothes against their limbs and sent plastic food wrappers and old newspapers swirling around them. The train shot out of the tunnel. Ryan turned to the boy. He looked to be a year or two younger than himself, maybe sixteen, with blond hair and green eyes. "You go to Benson High?"

The boy nodded. "My first day."

Ryan tapped him on the arm and nodded to the escalator. He started towards it and the boy followed. Behind them, the train slowed, brakes squealing, and stopped. The double doors on each car whooshed opened. A handful of glassy-eyed commuters stepped out. They stepped around the body of the teen lying on his back on the platform without a second look.

Ryan and the boy rode the escalator up. The boy said, "Dude, if he had connected, you'd have gone down on the tracks."

"I know. That train would have run me over and I'd be dead right now. It wouldn't bother him none. He'd brag about it to his homeboys."

The boy pulled out his phone. "I'll call the police."

"No, don't do that."

"But it was self-defense and I'm a witness."

"Doesn't matter," Ryan said. "I'm white and he's black. They'll call me a racist and throw me in jail." He saw confusion on the boy's face and said, "I'm serious, man. That's how they operate here. I'm not going to jail for defending myself. Put that phone away and don't tell anyone what you saw either."

The boy pocketed his phone. They reached the next platform and walked to the elevator.

"Where are you from?" Ryan asked.

"Kansas."

The elevator doors opened and the two boys stepped inside. A black man stood huddled and grunting in the corner of the elevator, his pants pulled down to his knees and his hand inside his boxer shorts, jerking wildly. Ryan and the

3

boy stepped out. The boy's face was pale. Ryan said, "You're not in Kansas anymore."

"I feel like I'm going to throw up."

"You'll see a lot of that if you ride the subway in this city."

"Don't they have cops down here?"

"Nah, man. People jerk off in the elevators, piss in the elevators, rob people in the elevators, nobody cares. If the cops arrest anyone, everybody cries racism. So nobody does anything."

They walked to the next escalator and rode it up.

The boy checked the time on his phone. "You're going to school early."

"So are you."

"They told me to come early for orientation."

Ryan snickered.

"What?" the boy said.

"Orientation."

"You did it?"

"Everyone does it. It's a two hour video on racism and white privilege. Then some teacher gives you a paper to fill out that says you apologize for being white and for being a racist and you promise to change. Don't sign it. Tell them you want to take it home and show it to your parents."

"Then what?"

"Then throw it away. If they ask you about it, tell them your parents still have it. Eventually, they'll stop asking."

"It sounds retarded."

"It is retarded. Everything here is retarded. They want you to feel guilty for being white."

"I don't want to go now."

"Just go, show up, pretend to listen to all their bullshit, and then as soon as it's over, forget everything they said and do the opposite."

The boy nodded. "Why are you going to school so early?"

"I come early a couple of days a week and hit the weight room. Then I do some reading in the library before school starts."

"They let you do that?"

"I don't tell anyone. I just slip in quietly through the gym doors and act like I belong there. The janitor sees me, he doesn't care."

"Based."

They rode the escalator up to street level and into the morning darkness on Hollywood Boulevard. Black men covered in tarps and ratty blankets were sprawled out on the sidewalk before them, sleeping. Ryan and the boy stepped carefully around puddles of urine and discarded needles. The boy frowned and pulled his shirt up over his nose.

"Smells like piss, doesn't it?" Ryan said.

The boy nodded.

"Welcome to L.A."

They walked west on Hollywood Boulevard. A fine mist covered the street and the cold morning air cut through the

5

stench and cleared Ryan's head. For the first time since the attack, he didn't feel his heart thudding against his chest.

"Don't flash money around here," he said.

"I know that much."

"And be careful what you say and who you say it to."

The boy nodded.

"Hold on a second." Ryan stepped past the boy to a newspaper bin on the corner of the sidewalk. He pulled open the plastic cover of the bin and pulled out a stack of X-rated papers. "I throw this crap in the trash whenever I see it," he said. He carried the papers to a nearby wastebasket and dumped them inside.

The boy watched. Ryan was taller than him, a good six feet, with a muscular build. "How much do you bench?" he asked.

"Two-sixty."

"Really? That's how you knocked that guy out."

"I bounce the weight a little. If you're talking super strict, then probably around two-forty."

"That's still a lot."

They passed more blanket-covered bodies sleeping on the sidewalk. One man sat with his back against a locked metal gate that covered the front of a gift shop. He babbled incoherently and drool dribbled from the corner of his mouth. A few yards down, the boys encountered another black man sitting on a bus bench. He turned to them as they passed and said, "Spare any change?"

The boys kept walking. Ryan said, "That guy has been panhandling on that same bench every day since I was in the fourth grade."

"Do you ever give them money?"

"No." A moment later, Ryan added, "Actually, there's an old black guy who panhandles on the subway. He's so bent-over and crippled he can hardly walk. Him, I give money to because I figure no one will give the guy a job. And kids. I see runaway kids around here all the time, thirteen, fourteen years old. I give them money, but they never ask. They're usually huddled up in a corner somewhere with a lost look in their eye."

The boy said, "We have trouble with blacks back in Kansas, but I never saw anybody try that Knockout Game before."

"You'll see it here. Be careful at school too."

"Really?"

Ryan nodded. "Some of them carry knives. Don't let anyone you don't know get behind you."

The boy said, "In Kansas a few years ago some black guy shot six people in the back of the head. Murdered them all. When they caught him he said he did it because he wanted to kill white people."

"They hate us, man."

"But why?"

Ryan shrugged. He didn't know the answer. The boy glanced at Ryan, thought for a moment, and said, "I went out with a black girl in Kansas." He saw Ryan stop walking and turn to face him. The boy added hastily, "Just a couple of times."

"You gotta be careful," Ryan said. "I mean, I understand the attraction. I like the exotic look myself, but what if she gets pregnant? You think some kid wants to grow up mixed race like that?"

"We never got that far."

"You would have, eventually. And then what, would you have married her?"

The boy laughed nervously. "I'm a long way from even thinking about getting married."

"Then you shouldn't be messing around with anyone."

"Are you serious?"

"I'm totally serious. This isn't a game we're living in. Don't date any girl you wouldn't consider for a wife. Don't date anyone you wouldn't want to have kids with. Don't date anyone who's stupid and immature."

They talked more as they walked. The boy's name was Jason. He showed Ryan his class schedule.

Ryan studied the list. "You're in my sociology class," he said. He looked at the list again and laughed.

"What?"

"You have science with Ms. Hope."

"Is she hard?"

"In more ways than one." Ryan saw the boy's questioning eyes and added, "She's a he."

The story was quickly told. Ms. Carline Hope was the school's science teacher. His real name was Scott Henson, but he came to school every day in a flaming red wig, red lipstick and a dress.

It had started a year ago when the school held a special assembly and announced that per California law, Education Section Code 220, all students and staff would now address Mr. Henson as Ms. Hope. Those who objected would be subject to counseling.

The girls didn't mind, they found it exciting. They brought balloons and home-baked cookies to school on the first day of Mr. Henson's "transition." The boys were different. Their attitude towards the science teacher ranged from disinterest to outright disgust, and the most disgusted ones of all were the black male students. They refused to call the teacher Ms. Hope; instead they called him Ms. Ho.

When they really wanted to rankle him, six or seven of them would wave their hands in class at the same time and call out, "Ms. Ho! Ms. Ho!"

Once when they'd done that, Ms. Hope broke down in tears and threatened to kill himself. The school went into lockdown, paramedics and police arrived, and it was several hours before order was restored. One of the black students present in class at the time summed it up best when he shook his head and said, "Damn drama queen."

The students involved in that incident were all written up, but nothing ever came of it. Esther Feinberg, the school

9

principal, waited three days and then shredded the disciplinary papers the boys had all signed. She didn't think it was fair to punish only black students even though they were the ones who caused the whole incident.

Instead the entire student body was forced to sit through a three hour transgender training program hosted by a bearded man in a dress that nobody paid any attention to, not even the girls who were bored with the whole affair now that the novelty had worn off and who spent the entire three hours focused on their phones.

Jason frowned. "Do I have to call him, Ms. Hope?"

He was surprised at the vehemence of Ryan's answer. "Don't call him anything. Don't even look at him. He wants attention. Don't give him any."

They reached the high school and exchanged phone numbers and email addresses.

"Good luck with orientation," Ryan said. "And be careful. Some of these girls at our school dress like hookers."

Chapter 2

Alone in the weight room, Ryan placed an Olympic bar on the uprights of his favorite bench and loaded it to 135 pounds. Now that football season was over, he had a bench press contest in mind. The contest was three months away and limited to lifters 18-years-old and younger. He knew almost all of the lifters would be juicing and he didn't think it was possible for him to win, but he calculated a strict 270-pound bench press would be good enough to take third place in his weight class. He lay back on the bench, tensed every muscle in his body, and popped the bar off the uprights. It felt light in his hands. He lowered the bar to his chest and pressed it back up for six smooth and easy reps.

The routine he devised was simple: a warm-up set with 135 pounds, followed by four sets of increased weight and descending repetitions of four, three, two, and one. He would train once or twice a week and add a pound and a quarter of weight to each end of the bar for his last three sets every workout. The tiny weight increases felt like nothing, and the low reps were easy to recover from and allowed him to build and consolidate strength. His top set today would be a single repetition with 245 pounds. By the day of the contest, his top set would be 270 pounds, maybe even 275 or 280.

He loaded a 25-pound plate to each side of the bar, raising the weight to 185 pounds, and nestled in underneath it. The weight popped up easy and he lowered the bar to his chest and pressed it up four times. He racked the bar with a clang that echoed through the room.

Between sets, he thought about the attack at the subway station. He felt a pang of remorse for breaking the boy's jaw, but then he remembered Jason's words: "Dude, if he had connected, you'd have gone down on the tracks," and he realized the boy who attacked him had actually tried to kill him. The thought of how close he came to death sent a shiver down his spine.

He knew the motive was race, but he didn't understand why it would prompt a complete stranger to try and kill him. He thought and he thought, but he just couldn't comprehend the reason behind such hatred. He felt the need to talk about it, to sort out the facts and discuss it with someone older and wiser. He decided to visit his uncle Frank, a counselor at the school, before his first class. Having made up his mind, he felt better. He loaded the bar to 205 pounds, laid back on the bench, and did three perfect reps.

Chapter 3

Frank Turner was digging deep into an overstuffed desk drawer in his office when he looked up and saw Ryan standing in the doorway. "Uh-oh," he said.

"Uh-oh, what?"

"You've got that look."

"What look?"

"That look you get when you're in trouble and you need me to bail you out."

"Nah, man. I'm cool. I just want to talk to you about something."

Frank waved to a chair in front of his desk and Ryan sat down. "Before you get started," Frank said, "how are you set on the wedding?"

"What wedding?"

"Uh, how many weddings are you invited to?"

"I don't know, you tell me."

Frank fidgeted and lowered his eyes. "Never mind."

Ryan leaned over the desk. "No, no, what wedding?"

"I guess she didn't tell you, huh?"

"Who didn't tell me what?"

"Your mother." He paused and added, "She's marrying Pierre."

"*Pierre?* She's marrying Pierre?"

The little Frenchman Pierre had been hanging around the apartment Ryan shared with his mother ever since she received an insurance settlement for the death of Ryan's father five months prior.

"Nobody told me anything," Ryan said. "When is this wedding supposed to happen?"

"Next month."

"Next month? She's marrying Pierre next month? Is he going to live with us, or do we have to live with him?"

Frank shook his head. "I have no idea, Ryan. You'll have to ask your mother."

"How come she didn't tell me this?"

"You'll have to ask her."

"We don't have room for him where we live. If he moves in with us, I'm moving out."

"How are you going to do that? You don't have a job."

"I'll get one. They can't marry anyway, he's not Catholic."

"He's not? She told me he was."

"She's lying. He's Lutheran or something. I told him once that if he didn't convert to traditional Catholicism he was going straight to hell when he died and he laughed, like it was a big joke." Ryan pushed himself out of the chair.

"Sit down," Frank said. "Relax."

"How can I relax when she's marrying that jerk? My dad's been dead less than six months and she's already remarrying? Aren't people supposed to mourn for at least a year?"

"It's typical female behavior, Ryan."

"And she doesn't even tell me. She doesn't tell me anything. I still don't know how much insurance money she got for my dad. I never saw a dime of it. Doesn't some of that money go to me? I'm so mad right now I could punch a hole in the wall."

"Not in my office, please."

"I knew she was fooling around with that jerk. I came home late one night and I saw him creeping out the front door of our building at two in the morning. So the next day I asked her about it, right? I said, 'Was Pierre here last night?' And she goes, 'Oh, no, he wasn't here.' She flat-out lied."

Frank shrugged. "It's typical female behavior. Study history, man. Study the Bible. The number of lying, scheming women in the Bible is legion. Nothing has changed. Human nature is the same now as it was then."

A thought occurred to Ryan and he said, "I'll bet she was doing this when my dad was still alive. I'll bet she was fooling around with Pierre the whole time my dad was sick and in the hospital."

Frank sighed and shook his head. "Look, she's my sister, but I have to call it the way I see it. She's horny, she wants sex. Men don't want to believe that women are that filthy, but they are."

Ryan turned and stormed out of the office.

Frank called after him, "Wait! What did you want to talk me about?"

Chapter 4

Jason sat at his desk and waited for science class to begin. His classmates were almost all Hispanic and almost all female and they seemed to have only one mode of dress: shorts and a halter top. The room was a sea of bare legs and bare midriffs with each girl prettier than the next. Outside of a public pool, Jason had never seen so much naked and exposed flesh. The girls were all focused on their phones. No one seemed to notice he was even there.

A tall Hispanic girl with jet black hair strode into the room dressed in a tube top and the tightest blue jeans Jason had ever seen. The girl seemed to be walking directly towards him and his eyes widened. He knew he was staring, but he couldn't take his eyes off her. She slid into the desk in front of him, her bare shoulders only inches from his eyes.

Jason's carnal thoughts were interrupted by a husky voice calling his name. He thought the voice came from a boy in class and he glanced around to see who it was. It wasn't until he heard his name called a second time that he realized the voice was coming from the front of the classroom. It was Ms. Hope, finger crooked, beckoning him to step forward.

The teacher had shaved hours ago, but the heavy makeup he wore failed to shroud the early morning shadow of his beard. Garish red lipstick covered his lips and an auburn-colored wig was perched crookedly atop his head. He sat behind his desk, waiting.

Jason rose out of his desk and approached his teacher. He felt his heart begin to pound against his chest. As a young boy he had been frightened of clowns and he felt that fear returning. He stood in front of the teacher's desk and tried not to stare.

Ms. Hope smiled and said, "Welcome to class." His deep voice made his appearance stand out even more.

Jason nodded.

"I checked your records," the teacher said. "It looks like science was one of your better subjects back at your old school. You should fit in here just fine. For today I want you to observe and familiarize yourself with how we do things. Understand?"

"Yes," Jason said.

The teacher's eyes were watching him intently and seemed to have come to a decision. "Yes what?"

"Yes, I understand."

"Yes, you understand what?"

Jason stared back at him dumbly.

The husky voice said, "My name is Ms. Hope."

Inwardly, Jason cringed. He remembered what Ryan had told him earlier that morning about not giving the teacher any attention, but this was his first day in class and his first day in a new school and he didn't want to cause trouble.

"My name is Ms. Hope," the husky voice said again.

Jason nodded. The teacher waited, then said, "Fine, we'll start over. I want you to spend your first day in class observing. Do you understand?"

"Yes," Jason said.

"Yes, *what?*"

Jason held his ground, said nothing.

"We can play this game as long as you want," Ms. Hope said.

Jason pretended to look puzzled. "I don't understand."

"Okay, maybe you don't. It's your first day, so I'll take your word for it. I want to hear you say my name. I don't think that's too much to ask. So, do you understand?"

Ms. Hope waited. Jason lowered his eyes and said, "Yes, I understand ... Ms. Hope."

"Good," the teacher said and his eyes held an odd sense of triumph.

Jason walked slowly back to his seat and slid in quietly. The girls around him were still on their phones. No one had paid any attention to his exchange with Ms. Hope. The girl sitting in front of Jason reached behind her head with one hand and pulled her long black hair up and over her shoulder, exposing her bare upper back and the back of her neck to his view, but Jason didn't care. Female skin was suddenly the last thing on his mind. He resolved then and there that at the first chance he got he was going to call his new science teacher Ms. Ho.

Chapter 5

Shelley Johnson, a skinny, pinch-nosed white girl in glasses stood in front of Ryan's sociology class with a sheaf of papers in her hand. On the blackboard behind her, written in bold white chalk, were the words *What Racism Means to Me*. Shelley cleared her throat and read from her papers with a squeaky voice. Her hands shook and the pages rattled as she read from them. "What racism means to me. As a white person, what racism means to me is white privilege, of which I benefit; of which *all* white people benefit."

Ryan glanced around the room. Most of the students were Hispanic. The ones who had already presented their reports looked bored. The others, the ones with reports still to give, looked tense.

Hector Martinez had been the first to give his report. He sat in the back of classroom, his bulky body slumped forward and his head down on his desk, snoring quietly. A small puddle of drool dribbled from the corner of his mouth onto the desk.

21

Shelley went on. "As a white person, I cannot expect to understand the full extent of my systematic and inherent racism. As a white person, I cannot expect to understand the immense grief and anguish my racism has caused for so many kind and gracious people of color."

There were two black students in class, a studious-looking boy in glasses and an overweight girl with weaves in her hair. They appeared to be paying attention, but Ryan wondered if they believed a single word they were hearing.

Brittany Parker, blond hair and blue eyes, sat up straight in her cheerleader uniform and glared at Shelley. The more Shelley droned on, the more rigid Brittany became. Ryan wondered if she feared being upstaged. Brittany was dating Marcus White, a black student and one of the school's top athletes. The young couple was conspicuous in their relationship, never missing an opportunity to hold hands or make out in the hallway. If any white person was free of racism, it was her. She stared harder at Shelley, her face strained with tension.

Brittany's cheerleader skirt, already short to begin with, had ridden up her thigh exposing almost her entire leg. Jason, one of only two sophomores in the class, sat to her right. Ryan watched him shift uneasily in his seat and steal a look at Brittany. Ryan nodded his head to get Jason's attention, but the boy didn't notice. He glanced at Shelley for a moment, pretended to pay attention, and then stole another hungry look at Brittany's bare white legs.

Ryan sighed. He turned to Lucy Ford, a short, snub-nosed blond girl with round cheeks who always sat quietly in the back of class, grabbing looks at her phone. She was doing that now, not even bothering to glance up occasionally and pretend to be paying attention. Lucy, Shelley and Brittany were the only white girls in the room. Hector Martinez, seated next to Lucy, snored louder.

Ms. Jodi Weidman, the sociology class teacher, sat in a school desk in the front row, her ledger book open before her and a grading pen in her hand. She was a squat woman, with short bobbed hair, glasses, and a drab face. She gazed up at Shelley with wide open eyes.

Shelley arched her back and lifted her chin. "I've judged African American people by the color of their skin and not by the kindness of their hearts. I've condemned people of color based on my own racist preconceptions and my own position of white privilege."

Shelley's nasally voice struck Ryan like fingernails on a blackboard. She sounded to him like a child telling her parents she'd just cleaned her room and expecting a cookie in return. He glanced again at Brittany Parker and he could almost see the steam coming from her ears.

Shelley shook the papers in her hand. "Like all white people, I am responsible for racism in America. Like all white people, it is *my* fault that people of color have struggled in our society. It is *my* fault that those whose voices are not heard are forced to protest in the street. It is

23

my fault that unarmed and defenseless young black men are murdered every day, every hour, on the streets of our city."

Ryan cringed. He could no longer understand a word Shelley was saying. The grating voice, the public groveling; it was all gibberish.

"I've been guilty; guilty of racism," Shelley said, and she lowered herself shakily to kneel on the floor. "And I kneel before you today, a person of privilege, a white person who has benefited from the structural and systematic racism of American society, guilty as ever. For this I am immensely humbled, for this I am immensely sorry. I ask your forgiveness. I ask you to forgive me and to forgive all white people for our sins and the sins of our ancestors. You are the ones who built our great cities, not us. You are the ones who built our country, not us. You are the ones suffering every day in America, not us. We stole your art. We stole your culture. We stole your inventions. We stole everything from you, while you sacrificed everything for us. You sacrificed everything so privileged white people like myself, and all white people could enjoy the benefits. I humbly and sincerely ask your forgiveness. The end."

Brittany Parker's face was stone cold. The rest of the class applauded politely. Shelley stood up, grinning, and walked back to her seat.

Ms. Weidman nodded her head. "Very good," she said. "Excellent." She penned a grade in her ledger book. "Now, who's next?" She consulted her student list and ran her pen down the column of names. There was disappointment in her voice when she said, "Ryan Turner."

Ryan rose out of his seat and walked to the front of the class. The words *What Racism Means to Me* on the chalkboard stood out in bold relief behind him. The room quieted.

Ryan glanced quickly at the faces of his classmates. In the back of the room, Hector Martinez was still sleeping. Lucy had her phone down and was watching him intently. Ryan looked her in the eye and said, "What racism means to me is being constantly on guard and attacked because of the color of my skin."

Ms. Weidman held up her hand. "Okay, I'm stopping you right there. That's never happened to you and you know it."

"It has happened to me," Ryan said, "many times."

The teacher slapped the desk with the flat of her hand. "No it hasn't. No one has ever attacked you for being white. Don't stand up there and claim otherwise." She turned to Brittany. "Has anyone ever attacked you for being white?"

Brittany shook her head. "Nope. Never."

"Me neither," Shelley said.

Jason raised his hand. "Ms. Weidman." The teacher turned his way. "This morning at the subway station," Jason said, intending to tell her of the assault he witnessed. He glanced quickly at Ryan before continuing. The older boy's cold stare silenced him and Jason's face flushed red. He lowered his hand. "Never mind."

Ms. Weidman turned back to Ryan. "Do you understand what this assignment is about?" Before Ryan could answer, she said, "This assignment is called *What Racism Means to Me*. It's an opportunity for you to confess your racism in a roomful of your peers and to ask their forgiveness."

"I'm not racist," Ryan said.

Loud guffaws filled the room. Malika, the overweight black girl with weaves in her hair, snickered. Jamal, the studious-looking black boy in glasses, chuckled and shook his head. Shelley Johnson smiled cheerfully and said, "All white people are racist."

"Speak for yourself," Ryan told her.

Confusion clouded Shelley's face. She turned to Ms. Weidman. "I thought all white people were racist."

"They are." Ms. Weidman nodded at Ryan. "He knows it. His refusal to acknowledge his racism is a sign of suppressed anger and denial." To Ryan, she said, "Sit down."

"What about my report?"

"I've heard enough of your report. I'm giving you an F."

A low murmur swept over the room. Ryan felt his face reddening. He remained standing in front of the class. Ms. Weidman pointed to his desk. "Sit down, I said."

Ryan walked slowly back to his seat.

Ms. Weidman said, "Class, your response?"

Jamal turned to Ryan. "You don't know what it's like to be pulled over because you're black."

"I've been pulled over," Ryan said.

"Not because of your race."

"How do you know?"

Malika rolled her eyes. Ryan noticed and said to her, "Seriously, how do you know?"

Jamal said, "I've been pulled over by the police for no reason, no reason at all, except because I'm black. You've never experienced that. No policeman has ever pulled you over because you're white."

"Did the cop tell you he pulled you over for being black?"

"Stop," said Ms. Weidman.

"No, it's a serious question," Ryan said. "If the cop didn't tell him he was being pulled over because he's black, then how does he know that?"

Jamal shook his head. "Man, you don't know anything."

"Did you get a ticket?"

"That's enough," said Ms. Weidman.

"You did, didn't you?" Ryan said to Jamal.

Ms. Weidman slapped her desk. "I said that's enough."

Ryan turned to her. "If he got a ticket then it means he was pulled over for speeding or doing something illegal." He said to Jamal. "Did you get a ticket?"

Jamal looked down at his desk and chuckled.

"You see?" Ryan said. "He did get a ticket."

Brittany spun around in her seat. "You don't know what you're talking about. You don't know what it's like for young black men in our society. You've never had a cop point a gun at your head."

"Yes, I have."

"When?"

"Last summer. There was a robbery down the street from my house. I was walking by and the cops all pointed their guns at me. Six of them. Handcuffed me too. I'm not crying about it."

Brittany scoffed. "That never happened."

"It happened," said Danny Lopez, a Mexican boy with high cheekbones and a thin mustache. "I seen it."

Ryan turned to him and the two boys exchanged a knowing look.

"I don't believe it," Brittany said.

Danny Lopez turned to her. "You calling me a liar?"

"Not you," Brittany said, "him." She nodded at Ryan.

"I just told you I seen it," Danny said.

"Right, so I believe you, but I don't believe him."

"How can you believe me and not him?" Danny said. "We're talking about the same thing. You either believe us both or you don't believe us both."

"Don't tell me what to believe," Brittany said. "I already told you: I believe you, I don't believe him."

Jamal turned to Danny and said, "What you're saying is your truth, and what she's saying is her truth."

"Thank you," Brittany said.

"Truth is truth," Danny said.

"Truth is relative," said Mr. Weidman. "We went over that last month. There is no one truth."

28

"Welcome to clown world," Ryan said, and several students laughed.

Ms. Weidman snapped at Ryan, "That's enough. As for this incident you claim to have happened, all it does is prove your white privilege. If you were black, you'd have been arrested or even shot."

"How do you know that?" Ryan asked.

"Duh!" Malika said. "It happens every day."

Ms. Weidman fixed Ryan with a cold stare. "African Americans are arrested in this country at a far higher rate than whites, Ryan. You know that. Don't lie and claim it isn't true."

Ryan said, "Maybe that's because they commit more crimes than whites."

Brittany Parker gasped. "That is not true," she said.

"It is true," Ryan told her.

"Now you're really lying," Jamal said.

"Hold on," Ryan said, "I brought some notes for my report." He reached in his shirt pocket and pulled out an index card. He glanced at Ms. Weidman, but she made no effort to stop him. The smug look on her face told Ryan she intended to give him just enough rope to hang himself.

Ryan read from the card. "Blacks make up thirteen percent of the population in the United States, but they commit over forty percent of the violent crime, including over sixty percent of the rapes and fifty percent of the murders."

Shelley's gasp was heard across the room. Heads turned her way and she fanned her face with her hand as if she were about to faint.

Ms. Weidman's voice was tinged with anger. "How dare you condemn a race of innocent people like that!"

"I'm not condemning anyone," Ryan said, "I'm just stating a fact."

"You're stating a lie," Brittany said.

"It's not a lie, it's a fact. And those numbers are just the ones who got caught. The actual numbers are probably a lot higher."

Jamal chuckled and said, "Those are hate facts."

"They're what?"

"Hate facts."

"What are you talking about, hate facts?"

"They're hate facts, they don't count."

"Of course, they count."

Jamal shook his head.

Ryan waved the card in his hand. "These are FBI crime statistics."

"They're hate facts."

"They're FBI crime statistics," Ryan repeated.

"They're hate facts. Look, you can wave that card around all you want, it doesn't change anything. They're hate facts, so they don't count."

"Since when do facts not count?"

"You're leaving out the context," Ms. Weidman said.

"What context?"

"Crimes committed in this country by African Americans have nothing to do with them. Their crimes are caused by systematic and institutional racism imposed on them by a racist white society."

"How is murder caused by racism?" Ryan asked.

"You see," Ms. Weidman said to the class. "He doesn't get it."

"You can't answer the question," Ryan said. "How are riots in Chicago caused by racism? How are busted out store windows and businesses being looted caused by racism?"

"That's not looting," Jamal said, "that's reparations."

"This is unreal."

"You really hate black people, don't you?" Jamal said.

"I don't hate anyone."

Several voices chimed in, "Yes, you do."

Ms. Weidman smiled. "Your racism is coming through loud and clear, Ryan."

"I'm not a racist, I'm a race realist."

"What does that mean?" Brittany asked.

"It means I realize people are different. Not better or worse, just different, and they want to be with their own kind."

Shelley gasped and said, 'That's racist."

"It's not racist at all," Ryan snapped. "It's reality." He turned to Jamal. "Would you like to live in a world without white people?"

"If the white people are all like you, then yeah."

The class burst into laughter. Brittany whooped and clapped her hands.

Ryan said, "So if all white people disappeared off the face of the earth – if you woke up tomorrow morning and we were all gone – would you be happy?"

"Hell, yeah."

The class laughed again.

Ryan turned to Malika. "Would you be happy?"

"Very happy," she said.

"All right, that's enough," Ms. Weidman said.

Ryan ignored her and turned to the Hispanic students. "Would you be happy to live in a world without white people?"

Most nodded their heads and said, "Yeah."

Hector Martinez woke up from his slumber in the back of the classroom, wiped the sleep from his eyes and the drool from his mouth and said, "They can give us back California, which they stole, and we'll make it Mexico again."

A couple of kids cheered and clapped.

Ryan said to Ms. Weidman, "You see, people want to be with their own kind."

"That's not true," Brittany said. "They just don't want to be around white people like you."

"No," Hector said, "we don't want to be around *any* white people."

Brittany looked at Hector aghast.

Ryan gestured to Jamal and Malika. "You guys can have New York, Miami and the east coast," he turned to the Hispanic students, "you can have California, Arizona and the west coast," he said to Jason and the three white girls in class, "and we'll take the Midwest and the northern states. Everyone's happy."

Several students burst into applause.

Ryan turned to Ms. Weidman and said, "You see? They want to be left alone, we want to be left alone, why can't everyone just be left alone?"

"It doesn't work that way."

"Why not?"

Ms. Weidman slammed her hand down on her desk. "Because it doesn't."

"But it's what everyone wants."

"I don't want it," Shelley said.

"Neither do I," said Brittany. She gestured with her hand at the students who applauded Ryan and said to him, "They're clapping because they don't want to be around racist white people like you."

"And you," Hector said.

Brittany gasped and spun around to face Hector. "How dare you say that? I'm dating Marcus White."

"That's why," Malika said.

Hector nodded at Malika and said to Brittany, "You stole her man."

Students laughed.

"I didn't steal anyone," Brittany said, "Marcus asked me out and I accepted."

"Maybe you should date homey here," Hector pointed to Ryan. "He's your color."

The class laughed loudly.

Brittany stared back at Hector. "You're racist too."

Hector grinned. "I'm Hispanic, I can't be racist."

"Don't you dare tell me who I can date," Brittany said. "I'll date whoever I want. I don't care what their color is."

"That's the problem," Malika said.

"Date whoever you want, girl," Hector said. "I'm just saying it ain't right."

Brittany turned to Ms. Weidman and her voice rose hysterically. "Are you going to do anything about this?"

"I let this go on," Ms. Weidman said, "because I thought it might be in the best interest of the class. Obviously I was wrong." She looked at Ryan. "Every time you open your mouth, you polarize the entire room."

"Nobody's polarized. Everyone agrees with me."

"Nobody agrees with you," Brittany said.

Ms. Weidman said to Ryan, "First, you lie and claim you're not racist."

"I'm not."

"Then you lie and claim you're attacked because you're white. Then you bring up a list of racist hate facts. Now it's mixed dating."

"I never said anything about mixed dating."

"Do you support it?"

"No."

Several girls gasped.

Ryan said, "Civilizations are destroyed by mixed dating."

Malika shook her head. "That's retarded."

Ryan ignored her and said, "Mixed dating is also selfish."

"How is it selfish?" Brittany demanded.

"It leads to mixed-race kids who feel like outcasts, because they don't belong to either side."

"That's ridiculous."

Valerie Buen, a brown-skinned sophomore girl with braided hair and arched eyebrows raised her hand. "No, he's right," she said. "I'm mixed. I'm Filipino and Mexican and I don't feel like I belong to either race. When I was little, both sides made fun of me."

Ryan glanced her way and Valerie returned his look.

Brittany said to Ryan, "I'm not having kids so don't call me selfish."

Ryan said, "Then you're having sex to have sex, which makes you the most selfish of all."

Brittany shrieked, "It's my body, my choice. I'm not having kids and I'm not getting married, so everyone just leave me alone." She faced the front of the room and folded her arms over her chest.

"Let's move on," Ms. Weidman said. She consulted her list. "Lucy Ford, you're next." As Lucy gathered up her notes, Ms. Weidman said to Ryan. "Your racism is abhorrent and you're dreaming if you think you or anyone else will ever be able to stop mixed dating and interracial marriage. That train has already left the station. There is no way to stop it. It can never be stopped and it never will be stopped."

"There is a way to stop it," Ryan said. "A very easy way, and if I was president I would stop it immediately."

Malika looked at him. "How would you stop it?"

The class fell silent and all eyes turned to Ryan.

Ryan said, "I'd sign an executive order that any girl found guilty of dating outside her race be publicly whipped."

There was a moment of stunned silence, followed by startled laughter from the boys and shrieks of outrage from the girls. Shelley Johnson sat with her lips quivering and her face drained of color. Brittany Parker leapt out of her seat and screamed hysterically at Ryan. Other girls joined her. Ms. Weidman stood up and raised her hands, trying to quiet them, but no one was listening. The entire class had descended into a pit of shrieking madness.

Jason watched with a stunned expression. Valerie Buen noticed and turned to him. "So," she said. "How do you like your first day at school?"

Chapter 6

Ryan was headed to his last class for the day when Danny Lopez pulled him aside in the crowded high school hallway and said in a hushed voice, "I got some news for you. Marcus White and his cousins are talking about jumping you on your way home from school today."

Ryan was instantly alert. "What'd you hear?"

"I was sitting at the table next to them at lunch and I heard Brittany tell him what you said in sociology class, about girls dating outside their race."

"Really? Marcus is mad about that?"

"At first he laughed," Danny said, "but that only made Brittany madder. She kept bitching at him about it, saying, 'A real man would do something about it. A real man wouldn't take that.' I could hear her at the next table. If some girl did that to me, I'd slap her. But Marcus just sat there, kept taking it. Finally, he told her to shut up. Then his two cousins were there and one of them said he knows the way you walk home from school. Anyway, I thought you'd want to know."

"Thanks, Danny."

"Watch out for Weidman too, man. That bitch is gonna flunk you."

"I don't care about her."

"I'm just saying."

"All right. Thanks, man." They shook hands and Danny disappeared into the throng of students in the hallway.

Ryan walked slowly to his class. He liked Marcus. They spent the previous summer running and lifting weights together to get ready for football. He couldn't believe Marcus would start a fight with him over something so stupid. Then again, if Brittany called Marcus out in front of his cousins, he might feel forced to respond just to save face. It was his cousins who complicated the matter.

Marcus' youngest cousin, Sam White, was a fourteen-year-old freshman. On his own, he posed little threat. But he was young enough and dumb enough to go along with anything his older brother, Trey White, proposed. Trey was seventeen, the same age as Ryan and Marcus. He was wiry thin, with hair that stuck out wildly in all directions, metal-capped teeth, and a scar on his cheek where someone once cracked a bottle. Trey had a long history of arrests for drug possession and fighting. There were even rumors that he'd knifed a kid last summer who was found dead at the mall up the street. Trey was the one most likely to start trouble.

Throughout his last class, Ryan stared down at his desk while his mind raced. He knew there would be no warning, no fair fight. They would strike from behind when he wasn't looking and there would be at least three attackers – they wouldn't risk an attack if they didn't outnumber him at least three-to-one. Depending on how many people Trey could recruit on short notice, there could be as many seven or eight attackers. They would swarm him from behind and try to drop him with a quick punch or two. Once he was down, they would follow up with a series of brutal kicks and stomps. Ryan had seen such attacks before. Often the original attackers would take off and complete strangers would join in, kicking the victim while they were down. If the victim was white, and he or she almost always was, it was practically guaranteed that other blacks, with no relation to the victim at all, would see what was happening and rush to jump in. At times there could be as many as twenty or thirty black attackers viciously beating and stomping on a single white victim. No arrests were ever made and no one ever went to jail.

The final bell rung and Ryan's class ended. He walked slowly amid the hurrying students in the hall to his locker and stowed all his books inside. If there was going to be trouble, he wanted his hands free to fight. He waited for the hallway to clear, and then walked quickly to the rear stairwell.

Normally he would exit from the front door of the school, walk north to Hollywood Boulevard and either hop on the subway at the corner of Hollywood and Highland, or walk a mile east past the shops which lined both sides of the street. If Marcus and his cousins were going to jump him, they'd likely follow him from the front entrance of the school and attack before he reached the corner of Hollywood and Highland. There was a mall at the corner and from there they could disappear into the crowd or duck into the nearby subway station.

Ryan's plan was to exit from the rear of the school, walk two miles out of his way in a circuitous route, and then double back to his street. He hustled down the empty stairwell, pushed open the doors at the bottom, and stepped into a small courtyard at the rear of the school. Lucy Ford was there, leaning back against a chain link fence, her eyes on her phone. She heard the door open and looked up.

"Hey," she said.

"Hey," he said back, and glanced anxiously around.

"What?"

"Nothing. Come on." He motioned for her to walk alongside of him and she eagerly accepted. They stepped through a gate at the rear of the school, past the guard in his little enclosure, and walked together down the sidewalk.

Lucy pocketed her phone and Ryan gave her a quick look. Standing this close she seemed shorter than she did in class. She was wearing blue shorts and Ryan noticed her legs were pale white and a little chubby, but well-shaped.

"I like what you said in class today," she told him.

"Really? You want to be whipped?"

"No!" she laughed. "The other stuff. All you were doing was telling the truth." She paused for a moment and said, "I only date white guys."

"Good for you."

He scanned the street ahead of them and glanced quickly over his shoulder.

"What are you doing?" Lucy said.

"Nothing, just want to make sure everything's all right."

"You're weird."

"Yeah, I know."

They walked along the sidewalk. He still wasn't sure anything was actually going to happen, but he felt safer walking with someone, even if it was a girl. The street they were on was quiet and the more distance they put between themselves and the school, the calmer Ryan felt. He said to her, "So what do you do when you're not in school?"

"I'm an anime girl."

"A what?"

"An anime girl." She stopped, pulled out her phone, and showed him a picture of herself dressed in a costume from a Japanese cartoon. "I go to these events, like parties and autograph signings. Here's one from a convention." She showed him another picture. "It's fun, don't you think?"

"Fun's not a part of my life."

"Really? Why not? You could do it. You could be a superhero. You're built like one."

Ryan grunted.

41

She showed him some more pictures. He pointed to one of her dressed in a blue super hero costume with matching blue hair. "Did you dye your hair for that?"

"No," she laughed, "it's a wig." She showed him another picture. "See, here's one of me with pink hair. I'm Emma from *Space Alien*."

"Right," he said, pretending to know what she was talking about. He thought she looked cute in the costumes, but he was repulsed by how revealing they were.

"People pay you for this?" he asked.

"Oh yeah," she said emphatically. "Some girls make a hundred thousand a year."

"A hundred thousand dollars? For this?" He pointed to a picture on her phone.

"Yup."

He thought for a moment and said, "That's kind of like being a whore, isn't it?"

"What? No!" She pulled the phone away.

"But who pays money for this?"

"People who are into it. Geeks and gamers, mainly."

"Well then it is like being a whore. You're selling sex, selling your appearance. Guys pay money, get excited, and jerk off to it."

"It's not like that at all," she said. "It's just for fun."

"Show me some more."

"No." She slipped the phone in her pocket. "I shouldn't have showed you anything. You're calling me a whore."

"I didn't say you were a whore. I said what you're doing is like being a whore."

Lucy's face flushed red with anger. "I'm no different than an actress or a model."

"They're the biggest whores of all."

Lucy turned and walked quickly away from him. He called out to her, "You don't have to sell yourself like that." She kept walking. He called to her again, "You're worth more than that." She flinched, ever so slightly, but kept walking.

Ryan looked both ways up and down the street. He was alone now and still not entirely safe. He would have to cross into a more populated area and that would increase the chances of his getting attacked.

A car passed and a black male passenger eyed him from the side window. Ryan's heart began to pound. He spotted a small diner in a strip mall at the corner and walked briskly towards it.

The diner was larger inside than it looked from outside. There were booths along the wall and half-a-dozen tables in the middle of the floor. A long L-shaped counter was lined with stools. Ryan crossed the room and took a seat at the far end of the counter. It was a perfect perch. It gave him a view of all the customers inside, along with the front door and the street out front.

A bored-looking white girl with a skeleton tattoo on her neck came to take his order. Ryan ordered an orange juice and turned his attention back to front door and the people inside. The room was half full. No music was playing, only a dull chatter among the customers.

The girl brought his juice and Ryan paid her with a five dollar bill. In the kitchen behind the girl, a sullen-looking cook frowned down at the food orders he prepared. Ryan decided he wouldn't stay long, just long enough to elude anyone who might still be looking to jump him.

When the girl returned, she plopped his change down on the counter in front of him and walked off without a word. She could at least thank me, Ryan thought, and he decided not to leave her a tip.

He took a sip of juice. It was cold, but sour and he knew it came straight from a carton and wasn't real orange juice. He sipped it anyway and kept an eye on the street outside and the front door. Three black teenage boys entered and sat at the far end of the counter, but they didn't look dangerous and Ryan didn't recognize them. They probably went to a different school. They were busy with their phones and paid him no mind.

Ryan leaned against the counter and watched. Minutes passed. The sense of danger faded. As he tilted his head back and drained the last drops of juice from his glass, he noticed the room was eerily devoid of conversation. Every customer was sitting with a phone in hand, neck hunched forward, staring intently at a screen. Behind him, a girl's voice whispered, "The people will not revolt. They will not look up from their screens long enough to notice what's happening."

Ryan spun around on his stool. Standing behind the counter was a pretty, thin-faced black girl. She was tall and slender with puffy black hair and a smattering of freckles across her cheeks and the bridge of her nose. He guessed her to be his own age.

"*1984*," Ryan said.

The girl's face lit up. "Oh my gosh, you know that!"

"Yeah, only it's not in the book, it's from a play based on the book."

He glanced behind her and saw that she was the only waitress on duty. The blond girl who brought his juice was gone. The sullen-looking cook was gone too, replaced by a smiling young black man in his early twenties. The new cook saw Ryan looking his way and waved. Ryan waved back. He noticed classical music playing softly over the sound system. The whole vibe of the diner was different and Ryan realized a shift change had taken place while he was drinking his juice.

"Really?" the girl said. "Are you sure?"

"I'm positive."

"Cause that's my favorite book and I thought it was in there."

Ryan shook his head.

The girl said, "I'll have to reread it. I think you're wrong."

"I'm never wrong."

"Ha. We'll see about that. Do you want some more juice?"

"No, I'm fine."

He suddenly realized his attention had been diverted and he snapped his head sharply back to the front door.

"You okay?" the girl said. "You look mad."

"I'm always mad."

"I like that," she said.

The black teens at the other end of the counter called for her. "I'll be right there," she told them. To Ryan, she said, "I'm impressed you know that quote. How old are you?"

"Seventeen."

She put up her hand and walked away. "Uh-oh. Too young for me."

Ryan watched her, the shape of her body and the way she walked. "Too young for what?" he called after her.

"Never mind."

"How old are you?"

She held up five fingers and flashed it four times.

"Twenty," he said to himself. He could have sworn she was his age, she had a young face.

The black teens had their phones down and were yapping with her. Ryan heard one of them say, "Come on, girl ... what's your number?"

Ryan watched her while pretending not to watch. When he stood up to leave, she came back.

"Seriously, you're only seventeen?" she said.

Ryan nodded.

"I thought you were older."

"I thought you were younger."

"Ha-ha. So when's your birthday? When do you turn eighteen?"

"March third."

"That's coming up."

"Yeah, if I live that long."

"Stop being so mad," she said, "you'll live longer."

He took a dollar from his pocket and his eyes searched the counter for a tip jar. He spotted it and stuffed the dollar inside.

"Thank you," she said quietly.

Ryan nodded and crossed the crowded floor of the diner. He braced himself for a possible attack and stepped out the door.

Chapter 7

Ryan glanced quickly left and right. He saw nothing suspicious and walked briskly down the sidewalk. He felt better now. With every step he felt more comfortable that nothing was going to happen. If Marcus and his cousins had planned to jump him, then most likely they had waited for him in front of school and his plan had fooled them. If not, then nothing was lost, only time. Tomorrow morning he would talk to Marcus alone and clear the air.

He covered two miles quickly, turned a corner onto his home street, and saw the shabby apartment building where he lived with his mother. He despised everything about the building - the broken light fixtures, the clogged plumbing - but seeing it brought him a sense of peace. He had made it home safe.

Six-year-old Talia Haddad sat on the top step of the stoop in front of the building. She saw Ryan approaching and immediately stood up. Ryan drew closer and smiled at her, but the little girl's face was serious. Ryan unlocked the six foot high metal security gate that surrounded the building and stepped through the entrance.

"I was waiting for you," Talia announced with a trace of admonishment in her voice.

"Sorry, Talia. I had some stuff to do at school."

She was a tiny girl with a somber face and a mass of wild black hair, a mix between her Mexican mother and Lebanese father. She perked up as he climbed the steps towards her. "Do you have a joke for me?"

"Maybe." He thought for a moment and said, "If hot and cold had a race, who would win?"

Talia grinned and shook her head. "I don't know."

"Hot would win," Ryan said, "because anyone can catch a cold."

The little girl laughed and he smiled down on her.

"Ryan," she suddenly blurted out, "I lost the crayons you gave me."

"Oh, well that's not good. I'll get you some more."

"Really?"

"Talia!"

It was her mother's voice, calling from their first floor apartment. Though Talia's family had lived in the building over a year, Ryan had never seen her mother. But he knew her voice well. Violent shouting often erupted from their first-floor apartment and echoed down the hall.

The mood of Talia's mother was instantly decipherable by the way she called her daughter's name. If she used a sing-song type of voice and drew the name out to three syllables – *Ta-li-a!* – it meant she was in good mood. If she called Talia's name sharply, as she did just now, it meant she wasn't.

A look of fear crossed the child's face. "I have to go," she said. Ryan opened the front door to their building and watched Talia run down the hall.

"You're my favorite," he called after her. It was a line she liked to hear from him and which never failed to make her smile. But the little girl did not respond.

Ryan watched her duck into the apartment at the far end of the hall, heard the door slam shut, followed by the grating voice of Talia's mother, scolding her daughter in Spanish.

Ryan frowned and climbed the stairs to his second-floor apartment. He slid his key in the lock and turned the knob. The door opened a foot wide and stopped. Cardboard boxes were stacked behind it. Ryan put his weight against the door and pushed, shoving the boxes back just enough to squeeze through the opening. He stepped inside.

It was a small apartment. His mother occupied the only bedroom and the cramped living room was packed with travel cases and handbags she sold online, along with piles of shipping boxes and computer equipment. The small sofa in the living room was covered with cases and handbags, leaving nowhere to sit except for the chair at his mother's desk. The boxes behind the door were orders waiting to be shipped.

Ryan closed and locked the door and slipped off his shoes. He was happy his mother wasn't home. The last thing he wanted to do was talk about her impending marriage to Pierre. There was no way Pierre could fit in their tiny, cluttered apartment. He turned on the light and looked into the hallway at the cot where he slept. There was a table beside the cot with an alarm clock, a reading lamp, and stacks of paperback books. He liked to lie on the cot and read late into the night. Next to the books was a hand-written card Talia had given him when his father died. Ryan considered the card his most prized possession.

On that night five months ago, heavy footsteps and the sound of men rolling a gurney down the hall had woken the little girl from her sleep and summoned her to peek out her door. Sensing that something serious and terrible had happened, she had crept up the stairs to the second floor and stood quietly, her little body rigid and her eyes wide, as Ryan's father was carried past her on a stretcher with a sheet over his head.

Two days later, she presented Ryan with a homemade card and the words I'M SORRY scrawled crookedly in crayon across the front. Ryan remembered hugging her bony body, feeling her little arms around his neck and his own tears running down his cheeks and he had resolved then and there that he would never, ever part with that card.

He stepped closer to the cot and saw a note propped up against his pillow. He picked up the note and read: "I have some business to take care of. I'll see you in the morning or tomorrow when you come home from school. I have a lot to talk to you about. Mom."

Ryan crumpled the note and threw it in the wastebasket.

Chapter 8

Marcus White was making out with Brittany in the crowded high school hallway, the two young lovers wrapped up together like a pair of fishing worms, when Ryan spotted him. Throngs of students passed without a look. To them it was a daily occurrence.

Ryan waited. He watched Brittany pull herself loose, give Marcus a quick, final peck, and disappear down the hall. Ryan scanned the hallway to make sure Marcus' cousins weren't watching and stepped out of the crowd. Marcus saw him approaching and his entire body braced. But then he saw Ryan smiling and Marcus smiled too.

"Hey, man," Ryan said. He extended his fist and Marcus bumped it with his own. "Just want to talk to you about something."

Marcus drew himself up. "Brittany says you dissed her."

"I didn't say anything to her personally. We were having a discussion about race in my sociology class and I said any girl who dates outside her race should be publicly whipped. I didn't mean her personally, and I didn't mean any disrespect to you. Mainly, I said it to get back at that dumbass teacher we have. She gave me an F on a report without even hearing it. Anyway, if that was disrespectful to you, I apologize. I wasn't thinking about you or Brittany when I said it."

Marcus nodded. "I thought it was something like that."

"So we're cool then?"

"We're always cool, bro. I ain't mad. Trey's the one that's mad."

"Can you talk to him?" Ryan asked.

Marcus shrugged. "I'll try, but you know Trey. He's got a thing for Brittany himself."

Ryan didn't know Trey, but the picture was becoming clearer by the second: Brittany was doing them both. At the very least, she was leading Trey on. Ryan suddenly remembered a conversation his parents once had about Brittany's mother, Debbie Parker. "She sleeps around," Ryan's mother had said. As a nine-year-old, Ryan didn't understand the comment. As a seventeen-year-old, he understood it perfectly. He realized it applied perfectly to both Mrs. Parker and her teenage daughter.

The crowded lunchtime cafeteria smelled of freshly baked pizza dough and pepperoni, but few students were partaking; they were too engrossed in their phones. Occasionally, a hand would slide over a paper plate, pick up a slice of pizza, and lift it to a mouth for a bite, but the other hand, the one holding the phone, never wavered. Neither did the eyes.

Ryan knew without even looking that every boy in the cafeteria was either playing a game on his phone or watching porn, and that every girl was either updating her social media profile or frowning with disapproval at the profile of a girl they were jealous of.

He spotted Lucy sitting alone at a table in the far corner of the cafeteria, staring intently at her own phone. He walked over, slid into a chair across from her and said, "Hey."

Lucy's eyes flicked up from her phone. "What do you want?" she asked sullenly.

"Just saying hey." He waited for her to speak, but she said nothing. Her attention was back on her phone. "Did you think about what I said yesterday?" he asked.

"No. I don't care about what you said."

"Can I ask you a personal question?"

"No."

"Are you religious at all?"

Lucy lowered her phone. "I said no." Her eyes returned to her phone.

"It's a simple question."

"I was raised Catholic, but I'm not now. I'm spiritual, but not religious."

Ryan scoffed. "What does that mean?"

"It means what it says. Why do you care?"

"I want to see you get to Heaven."

"Who says I'm not going to Heaven?"

"Based on those pictures you showed me yesterday, I'm not so sure."

"There's nothing wrong with my pictures."

"You're tempting guys to sin."

Lucy glared at him over her phone. "No, I'm not."

"Yes, you are. If an adult gives a pair of scissors to a two-year-old and the kid cuts himself, whose fault is it?"

"That's not the same."

"It is the same."

"Adults aren't two-year-olds."

"When an adult male sees skin on a girl, he becomes a two-year-old."

"That's not the girl's fault."

"Sure, it is. Look at it this way: If someone is poisoned, who's guilty of murder – the person who drank the poison or the person who prepared the poison and gave it to him?"

"That's not the same."

Ryan sighed. "You don't understand what I'm saying."

Lucy set her phone down on the table. "I understand what you're saying, but it's like you're trying to blame girls for guys being horny."

"Who made them horny?"

"They made themselves horny! You make it sound like guys have no control."

"You have no idea what it's like."

"And you think actresses and models are whores?"

"They're human scum."

Lucy shook her head and picked up her phone.

Ryan swept his arm in an arc to indicate everyone seated in the cafeteria. "All these girls you see here dressed in their skimpy outfits; they're all going to hell when they die. The girls you see on the internet, posing and showing skin, they're going to hell too. Actresses, models, all of them. And you know who else is going? All the guys sending them money and jerking off to their pictures."

"You don't know that."

"I do know that."

"No, you don't."

"Okay, I'm not one hundred percent sure, but I'm ninety-nine percent sure."

She stared at him. "You ... are ... weird."

"You told me that yesterday."

Lucy looked at her phone. "I don't believe in hell."

"You'll believe it when you get there."

Lucy looked up at him and said, "You do it."

"Do what?"

"I've seen you wearing tight shirts before, showing your muscles."

"That's not the same."

"Yes, it is. How is it different than a girl showing her body? You're tempting people to sin just like they are."

Ryan stared down at the table. "Okay," he said. "Point taken. I won't do it anymore."

"That's a laugh."

"I'm serious, I'm not doing it. I'll never wear a tight shirt in public again."

Lucy's attention shifted from Ryan to something behind him and her eyes widened in panic. Ryan noticed and spun around. He saw Trey White running in a crouch towards him, his eyes bloodshot and wild, holding a chair in his hands. Running close behind Trey were Sam White and another black teen. The surprised look on Trey's face betrayed his intentions. He had planned to slam the chair into Ryan's head while his back was turned, but now Ryan had spotted him. In a panic, Trey lifted the plastic chair overhead and threw it. Ryan ducked and covered his head. The chair flew past him, hit the table and bounced up over Lucy's head. She screamed. Students across the cafeteria looked up from their phones.

Ryan leapt to his feet and backed up. Trey, Sam and the black teen rushed him. Ryan grabbed the nearest chair and hurled it at the three of them. Trey stumbled over the chair and spilled to the floor. Sam stepped around his cousin, tip-toeing and arms out for balance. Ryan closed the gap and threw a punch at Sam's jaw. His fist landed with a crack that sounded like two pool balls hitting. The boy dropped to the floor. Then the entire cafeteria came alive. Kids leapt from their seats and rushed each other throwing punches. At a nearby table, a black student Jason had never seen before ran up to him from behind and punched him in the side of the head. At another table, Danny and two friends were attacked by rival Hispanic kids. An obese black girl punched the face of an obese Hispanic girl and grabbed her by the hair. Groups of girls hurled food trays and soda cans at each other. Others screamed and ran for the exits, stepping over tables and trampling anyone in their way. Security guards blew whistles and shouted over the din.

Ryan turned to the black teen behind Sam. The boy's eyes grew wide. He backed up and ran away. Trey was back on his feet and stumbling forward. Ryan swung at him and missed. Trey swung back. His fist caught Ryan high on his cheekbone, just below his eye. Ryan staggered back, his head spinning. Trey swung again. Ryan slipped the punch and grabbed his attacker. The two of them fell to the floor, grappling.

Ryan slipped his arms under Trey's arms and clasped his hands behind the boy's neck, catching him in a full nelson. He lifted Trey's head and slammed it into the cafeteria floor with a dull thud again and again. On the third thud there was blood on the floor and Trey had stopped struggling.

Ryan released Trey and left him unconscious on the floor. He stood up. Fights raged all around him. He heard the crack of fists against flesh, the sound of tables being overturned, and the whistle of chairs flying overhead. He spotted Jason curled up in a ball on the floor. Two black teens stood over him, kicking and stomping at his head. Valerie Buen stood nearby screaming at them to stop.

Ryan picked up a chair and charged the two boys. He rammed the chair into the face of the closest one. The chair cracked the boy across the teeth and he staggered back, then both boys turned and ran.

Ryan and Valerie each grabbed Jason by an arm and pulled him to his feet. They hustled him towards the exit. Ahead of them, a heavyset black girl had Lucy by the hair with one hand and was swinging with her other hand, trying to connect with a punch to the head, but mostly missing. Ryan shouted, "Let her go!" and rushed over. He grabbed the black girl's arm, twisted her grip off Lucy's hair and shoved the girl away. Then he took Lucy by the arm and pulled her towards the exit. Valerie and Jason followed.

Chapter 9

It took several hours for school officials and the security staff to go over the surveillance video from the cameras in the cafeteria and take statements from everyone involved. It was clear that Trey, Sam, and the third teen boy had started the fight, but Esther Feinberg, the school principal, didn't think it was fair for only black students to be punished and she refused to expel them. Instead, she pressed to expel Ryan and only relented when Frank convinced her that such an action would lead to a lawsuit. Feinberg's final decision was to suspend for two days every student who was present in the cafeteria at the time of the fight and to order all of the school's white students to attend diversity training.

Trey was the only student seriously injured and he was taken to the hospital with a fractured skull. The cameras didn't catch Ryan slamming Trey's head into the floor when the two boys were wrestling and Ryan didn't volunteer the information.

Nothing at all happened to Brittany Parker.

Talia was waiting on the steps in front of their apartment building when Ryan returned home from school. She saw the bruise on his cheek and his half-closed eye and she stood up with alarm. "What happened to your eye?"

Ryan unlocked the metal gate and stepped through it. "I fell down," he said.

"I don't believe you."

Ryan laughed at her candor. "Why do you say that?"

"Because my mom gets that." Talia balled her fingers into a tiny fist and smacked it into her open hand.

In a moment of instant clarity, Ryan knew why he never saw Talia's mother. She was too embarrassed to be seen by her neighbors with a battered face and a black eye.

Ryan's cheek and the entire side of his face throbbed with a sharp, pulsating pain, but he lied and said, "It's okay. I'm feeling better already."

The little girl's face was etched with concern. "Can I get you something?"

"No, but thanks for asking."

He told her a joke, which brought a smile to her face, and they talked until Talia's mother called for her and she ran down the hall to her apartment.

When he entered his own apartment, his mother leapt from her desk and shrieked. "What happened to your eye?"

"I got in a fight."

"With who?"

"Somebody at school."

She reached for his face and he pulled away.

"Come here," she said.

"No, mom, I'm fine."

"Come here, I want to see your face."

"No," he insisted and stepped past her to the bathroom. He stepped inside, closed and locked the door, and looked at his reflection in the mirror.

His mother's voice carried from the other side of the door, "What were you fighting about?"

"Nothing." He touched the purple bruise high on his cheek and winced.

"Don't tell me 'nothing'," his mother said. "You were fighting about something."

"It's no big deal."

"It *is* a big deal. What did the school say?"

"I'm suspended for two days."

"You *what?*" The doorknob rattled. "Open this door."

"No, mom. Go away. I'm fine." He turned the water on in the sink as loud as he could to drown out her voice.

The doorknob rattled again followed by loud knocks on the door.

Ryan ignored them.

Ryan stared down at the plate of macaroni and cheese on the table before him. He speared a chunk with his fork and popped it gingerly between his lips. It tasted warm and sticky in his mouth and with each movement of his jaw the pain in his cheek deepened and throbbed.

His mother sat at the table across from him. "I'm getting married," she said guardedly. "Next month. To Pierre." She waited for him to speak, but he said nothing, stared down at his plate and chewed. "Don't you have anything to say?" she said.

Ryan shook his head.

"You could at least say something."

He shook his head again. He was waiting for the really bad news - that Pierre would be moving in with them.

"How can you sit there and not say anything?"

Ryan kept his head down and said, "It won't be valid."

"What are you talking about?"

"Pierre's not Catholic, so the wedding won't be valid."

"Stop with that, all right?"

"It's true."

"I don't care. I don't want to hear it."

"You want to go to hell?"

"Stop," she said.

He stopped. He was through trying to help her. He was through trying to help everyone. Except Talia. He would help her, if he could. And Lucy. And maybe ...

His mother's voice interrupted his thoughts. "There's something else we need to talk about. After the marriage, I'm moving in with Pierre."

Ryan's eyes flickered. He felt his pulse quickening.

"He has a spare bedroom," his mother said. "You're welcome to use it, but you're turning eighteen soon, so it's up to you whether you want to live with us or not. Pierre lives in West L.A., so you'll have to take a bus to school every day and back."

Ryan looked up for the first time. "Can I stay here?"

His mother shook her head. "It's too expensive."

"I can get a job."

"You have to finish school first."

"I can do both."

"That's complicated," she said.

"But if I can do it, I can do it, right?"

"We'll see."

His mother looked doubtful, but in Ryan's mind it was a done deal. He'd work two jobs if he had to. He'd do whatever it took.

"Anyway," his mother said, "it's going to be a small ceremony. Just a few friends. We'd like you to come, but I know you're busy so don't feel like you have to."

"I can't go to a non-Catholic wedding."

"It's in a church."

"Pierre's not Catholic."

"Will you stop with that?"

"And the priest isn't valid either, unless he was ordained in the early 1960s."

"Enough," his mother shouted.

"I'm just telling you."

65

"Fine. Whatever then. Come, don't come, it's up to you. I'm through with this conversation."

They chewed the rest of their food in silence.

Chapter 10

His mother left the apartment when they finished eating and Ryan knew he wouldn't see her until morning. There was a footlocker under his cot where he stowed his socks, underwear, and a few shirts. From it, he pulled an old T-shirt he no longer wore. He laid the T-shirt on the kitchen counter, packed it with ice cubes, and folded it over itself. Then he lay back on his cot, held the makeshift ice pack to his cheek, and stared up at the cracks in the ceiling.

He thought about the fight at school and he hoped the worst of it was over. But he wasn't sure. Trey might get out of the hospital and come looking for him. He'd have to be careful. He'd have to keep an eye out not to get knifed in the hallway at school.

He'd have to keep an eye out for Marcus too. If he wasn't mad before, he would be now. Then again, with Trey out of the picture, Marcus would have Brittany all to himself. Maybe Marcus didn't mind Trey going to the hospital. Maybe everything would blow over.

Ryan thought about Lucy. After he'd pulled her out of the cafeteria, she'd run away crying and he hadn't seen her since.

He thought about the black girl he met at the diner the night before; the freckles on her face and the sound of her voice, and he decided to pay her a visit on the first day of his suspension.

Music was playing and lively chatter filled the air when Ryan stepped through the door of the diner. All of the booths and tables were occupied, along with most of the stools along the L-shaped counter, but the seat at the far end of the counter, the one where Ryan had sat the last time, was open. He headed for it.

The young black man in the kitchen spotted him immediately. He smiled and waved as Ryan slid onto the stool. Ryan waved back. The black girl was there, bustling about, taking and delivering orders. Ryan watched her until she spotted him and approached. Her smile disappeared when she saw his eye and the dark bruise on his cheek.

"Oh my gosh," she said. "What happened?"

"You remember me?"

"Of course, you're the *1984* guy. What happened?"

"I got into a little scuffle at school."

"It looks like more than a little. Are you okay?"

"I'll live."

"Ha-ha. Wait, do you go to Benson?"

Ryan nodded.

"That was on the news," she said. "They called it a race riot."

"Pretty much."

"Who started it?"

Ryan paused a moment and said, "I guess I did."

"*You?*"

Ryan made a flippant gesture with his hand. "I said something a couple of days ago that pissed off this girl and then the girl told her boyfriend about it and then the boyfriend's cousin started the fight."

"I knew it."

"Knew what?"

"I knew there was a woman involved."

Ryan laughed. "How did you know that?"

"There always is. Are the boyfriend and the cousin who started the fight black?"

"Actually, yeah."

"See? I knew that too."

"But how?"

"From the way you described it."

A customer called for her. She moved down the counter and called to Ryan over her shoulder, "Did you want something?"

"Just some orange juice," he called back.

He watched her wait on customers; watched the other customers around him. Everyone looked happy. It was as if the girl and the smiling young cook in the kitchen infected everyone with their energy. He had noticed it before, in his first visit a few days ago.

The girl brought his juice. He reached in his pocket for money, but she waved him off. "It's on the house – me and Thomas." She waved her hand to indicate the young cook in the kitchen.

"Really?" Ryan said. "Thanks." He waved his hand in appreciation to Thomas. Thomas smiled and nodded.

More customers came in. Others formed a line outside the door, waiting for an empty table or seat. The customers kept the girl busy, but whenever she had a spare moment, she returned to Ryan.

He told her in bits and pieces about the fight in the cafeteria and his life at school and he told her that because of the fight in the cafeteria he and every other white student in the school would have to take diversity training. "Oh gosh," the girl said. "Don't do it. That's so stupid." At one point, she looked him in the eye and said, "You still haven't told me the most important thing of all."

"What's that?" Ryan asked.

"What you said that made this girl so mad she told her boyfriend about it and made his cousin start the fight."

Ryan squirmed in his seat. "I'm not so sure I should tell you that."

"Why not?"

"You might get mad."

"I won't get mad. I promise."

Ryan studied her face. He decided to tell her. "I said any girl who dates outside her race should be publicly whipped."

The girl took a step back. "Oh no, you didn't."

"Oh yes, I did."

"Do you believe that?" she asked.

"To a point."

"What do you mean 'to a point'?"

Ryan wondered if he should be completely honest with her. He chose to be half honest. "I mean if two people really like each other then they should hang out together. But that's not how it is with most people."

"How is it with most people?"

"Most people who date outside of their race do it because they're horny and it's convenient. Or they do it to be different and show off. I guess it's the whole hookup culture that I really disagree with."

"I don't hear many guys talk like you," she said.

"Some people say I'm weird."

"I can see why."

Ryan laughed.

"So are you saving yourself for marriage?" she asked him.

"I'd like to."

"But are you?"

"I'd like to," he said again.

"You don't believe in any sex outside of marriage?"

"No."

"Wow. So if you see a pretty girl, you don't get tempted?"

"Of course, I get tempted. I get tempted out of my mind. But I'm not going to hell over a quick fling with a girl. I don't care how good-looking she is."

Customers called for the girl. She took another step back and said, "Are you Catholic?"

"Yeah."

"I knew it," she said, and hurried down the counter.

"You know everything," Ryan said quietly, but the girl didn't hear.

Minutes passed, Ryan sipped his juice. Customers kept coming in and lining up at the door and the girl no longer had time to talk to him. He stood up to leave. A customer waiting by the door saw Ryan stand and immediately walked over to take his seat. "Hold on," Ryan told him.

He waited for the girl to spot him. When she did, she hurried over and he thanked her again for the juice.

"Wait," she said. She grabbed a small towel from under the counter, filled it with ice cubes and folded the ends of the towel over the ice. She handed it to him with a smile.

Outside, the night air felt crisp and clean. Ryan held the makeshift icepack against his cheek as he walked. He was twenty feet down the sidewalk when he suddenly stopped and punched his thigh. He had forgotten to ask the girl her name.

Chapter 11

The sky hung over the high school with a gray pallor and a heavy rain hammered the asphalt parking lot and pelted the roofs and hoods of the cars parked there.

Frank leaned back in his office chair and fixed Ryan with a steady gaze. "It's diversity training," he said. "There's no test, no quiz. Just go, show up, pretend to listen to all their bullshit, and then as soon as it's over, forget everything they said and do the opposite."

Ryan lowered his eyes, smiled wryly and shook his head. It was the same advice he had given Jason about orientation a few days before.

"What?" Frank said.

"Nothing."

"Look, you have to go, Ryan."

"I don't have to do anything."

"If you want to graduate, you have to go."

"Then maybe I won't graduate."

"Get serious."

"I am serious. I didn't start the fight; all I did was defend myself. Why do I have to go to diversity training?"

"Because that's what the warden wants." Frank glanced at the clock on the wall. "Aren't you supposed to be in sociology class right now?"

Ryan shrugged.

"So it's your first day back from suspension and already you're cutting class?" Frank shook his head. "I don't know why I bother, man. Fighting with these idiots to keep you from getting expelled.... Yeah, they wanted to expel you."

"I wish they had."

Frank started to speak, thought better of it, and started again. "Did you know that there are three factors that almost guarantee a person will succeed in life? It's true. A study came out a few years ago. They came up with three factors that almost guarantee a person will succeed in life and end up either in the upper class or middle class of society. Only two percent ended up in poverty. Two percent. Do you know what those three factors are?"

Ryan folded his arms across his chest, waiting.

Frank said, "The first factor is *finish high school*. The second is get a full time job. The third is don't get married and have kids until you're in your twenties. According to the study, any person who does those three things is almost guaranteed to succeed in life. I could add two more – avoid criminal behavior and save as much money as can. But even without those extra two, just with the first three factors alone, a person has only a two percent chance of failing in life. And here you want to piss it all away when you're only four months away from graduating."

"You don't understand," Ryan said. "I've had it. I don't care about finishing high school anymore. I just don't care."

"Well that's pretty stupid."

"I can get a GED."

"It's not the same. I mean, it is the same, but it's not the same."

"Do you really think somebody hiring me for a job is going to care whether I graduated or whether I have a GED?"

"If you want to work in academia, I can assure you they will care." He saw the frown on Ryan's face and said, "I guess you don't want to work in academia. Look, I understand your frustration."

"No, you don't."

"Yes, I do. And let me tell you something, you think you have it bad, sitting in class with your teachers for six hours a day? I have to work with these retards. Every one of them, dumb as a rock, and I mean that literally." He pointed to an empty chair next to Ryan. "I could put a rock in that chair and a teacher from this school in the chair where you're sitting and the rock would be smarter."

Ryan laughed.

"I'm serious," Frank said, "and you know I'm serious. This isn't what I signed up for. My mission in life was to teach young minds, to get them excited about learning, excited about making a difference in the world. Instead, I spend half my time here explaining to teenagers who can't read or write why the education system has failed them, why the law requires them to pretend some dude in a dress is really a woman, and why the world isn't going to end in ten years because of some stupid global warming bullshit. You should see the looks on their faces when I tell them that last one." He dropped his jaw and bugged his eyes in imitation. "At first, they think I'm joking, but then I show them the data and the science and that's when they get mad. They want to know why their parents lied to them, why their teachers lied to them. Then what am I supposed to say? Uh, your parents are fools and your teachers are all liars?"

Frank went on, "You should see these parents when they come in here. They want to know why their tenth grade daughter is failing fourth grade math, why their twelfth grade son is reading at a third grade level. All day long I'm dealing with this."

"What do you tell them?"

"I tell them the truth. 'Your child's teachers are losers. Your child's teachers are lazy, worthless, and stupid, and they have no interest in seeing your child succeed in life.' That's what I tell them. But then instead of getting mad at the teachers or the teachers union, they get mad at me." He reached for a notepad on his desk. "Listen, I want you to go to your sociology class. I'll write you an excuse note for being tardy."

Ryan squirmed in his seat. "Just let me skip this one time. I'll show up tomorrow. I promise."

"You act like this class is torture."

"It *is* torture. The teacher has it out for me."

"Not every teacher in this school has it out for you, Ryan."

"This one does."

Frank set the notepad back on his desk. "This teacher that gives you such a hard time, this Jodi Weidman, she might be doing it to get back at me."

"You?" Ryan sat up straight. "Why you?"

"We were at a teacher's conference in Sacramento a few years ago. She was drunk and gave me her phone number. Then an hour later she was even drunker and asked me to go back with her to her hotel room."

"Are you serious?"

Frank nodded.

"Did you go?"

"Are you kidding? I told her I wasn't feeling well and then I went back to my own room, locked the door, and tore her phone number into a million pieces. She's been trying to get me fired ever since."

"How long has this been going on?"

"Two years. At first she told everyone I was gay. I was so mad I could have killed her, but it turned out to be a good thing, because later when she tried to get me fired, they couldn't do it, because gays are a protected class."

"Does anyone here know you're not gay?"

"I think they all know. I'm pretty sure Feinberg knows, but there's nothing anyone can do about it. Jodi outed me and if anyone tries to push me on it, it's harassment of a protected class. I've hinted that if they try anything, I'll get a lawyer and sue them all. Now listen, you can't repeat this to anyone, and I mean anyone."

"I won't," Ryan promised.

"I'm serious, Ryan."

"I won't tell anyone," Ryan said emphatically.

"So you see, I think the reason she gives you such a hard time is to get back at me. And if you drop out and don't graduate, it's like she's won."

"That *bitch*."

"It's typical female behavior, I told you before."

"I know, read the Bible."

"It's all in there. I'm not talking about Mary – she's sinless – or her mother Anne, or some of the others, but look at all the lying, scheming harlots in there. Look at Eve. She had it all, living in the Garden of Eden. No woman in history ever had it so good. So what does she do? She goes and does the *one* thing that God specifically told her not to do. Then she tricks Adam into going along with her and gets him to do it. That right there tells you everything you need to know about most women. And Adam, getting duped and going along with her; that tells you everything you need to know about most men."

"This is all so damn depressing."

"Listen," Frank said, "let me fill you in on one of the great secrets of life. Are you ready?" Ryan nodded. Frank leaned over his desk, lowered his voice to a conspiratorial tone and said, "Men build societies, women destroy them. Never forget that. Men are the inventors, the creators, the great romantics. Women are none of those things. They're nurturers. They're meant to be mothers and when they don't get married and raise children like they're supposed to, they project their mothering instincts onto all the victim groups of the world: rioters, looters, homos, illegal aliens, refugees, communists, you name it, all the enemies of society. That's how societies are destroyed. Do you understand?"

Ryan nodded.

Frank went on. "The sad truth is if it wasn't for sex, most men wouldn't spend any time around women at all. We all know it, but we pretend otherwise. Plus, we're men; we have an overpowering need to procreate, to have sex. It's in our genes and there's nothing we can do about it. But we can't have sex outside of marriage or it's whoosh," he made a flippant gesture with his hand, "straight to hell. Jerking off, same thing, whoosh," he made the same gesture with his hand, "straight to hell again. So we look for women to marry, to raise families with, and what do we find? Nothing but a bunch of fat, tattooed, purple-haired whores. And the worst ones of all, the absolute worst ones," he pronounced the words very carefully, "are left-leaning white women."

He paused for a moment to let his words sink in. "These stupid bitches - these left-leaning white women - are wrecking the country every day, every single day, and we're left dealing with the fallout from all the messes they create. Constantly, man ... constantly cleaning up their messes. You know, it's amazing. No other race does to their young what the left-leaning white woman does to hers. Blacks don't do it. Asians and Hispanics don't do it. But white women, the ones that vote Democrat, the ones that support the riots and the looters and vote against their own race? Forget it." He adopted a tone of female mimicry in his voice. "Abort our babies, rape our little girls, sodomize our little boys and turn them into faggots and trannies, we don't care. Just don't call us racist."

Frank shook his head. "No other animal does that. You try messing with a lion cub or a bear cub and watch what happens. That mama lion will tear you to pieces. That mama bear will eat you for lunch. Dogs, cats, ducks, birds, they're all the same. But left-leaning white women? They don't care. Despite having every advantage and privilege in the world, despite having Mary, and St. Anne, and St. Theresa and all the other saints throughout history as guides and role models for how they should live their lives, despite all that and more, they've become the most vile, the most disgusting, the most despicable life form on the planet."

Frank leaned back in his chair. "Now all this talk about women I give you, it doesn't mean you can't find a decent girl somewhere and get married. I mean, it's doubtful, but it's not impossible. Somewhere in the cold reaches of space a decent girl might exist, but not in this city. The women here have been brainwashed beyond repair. And I hate to say it – I really hate to say it – but you might be better off with a nice Hispanic or Asian girl. They tend to be more traditional, and they age better too. Especially the Asians. But you have to find one that's not a stupid bitch."

There was a quick knock on the door. It opened and Margi Holland, a fellow counselor stuck her head inside, her eyes wild and her face flushed.

"What is it?" Frank asked.

"It's Ms. Hope," said Margi, "she's trying to kill herself."

"Again?"

Margi nodded. "The boys in her class were calling her Ms. Ho and she freaked out. She's in the women's restroom on senior hall. She has a razor blade and she says she's going to slit her wrists."

Frank rose out of his chair and Ryan rose with him. "You stay here," his uncle said.

"Are you kidding? This I gotta see."

"I said stay here." It was a command and Ryan sat down. Frank said to Margi, "Make sure he stays in my office." Margi nodded. "Did you call security?" Frank asked her.

"Not yet, I wanted to tell you first."

Frank stepped out of his office and moved swiftly past a row of administration offices. He stepped out of the administration department into an empty hall, climbed the stairs to the second floor, and strode quickly down the hall. Ahead of him, a gaggle of girls were huddled outside the women's restroom. They had the door cracked open and were peeking inside.

Brittany Parker stood close by, filming herself with her phone. "Hey guys, I'm live from school in a really tense situation. One of our teachers is barricaded in the women's restroom and is threatening to kill herself with a razor blade. This is like the most terrible thing that's ever happened to me in my life and I really need your support, so please subscribe to my channel and send me a donation. All donations of a hundred dollars or more will receive my latest bikini and lingerie pictures. These are really hot pictures, guys. I wouldn't kid you. And now ... back to the suicide."

Frank's voice bellowed down the hall. "Get away from that door."

The girls scattered like a flock of frightened hens only to regroup behind Frank. "Get back to class," he told them. He turned to Shelley Johnson. "Where's your teacher, where's Ms. Weidman?"

Shelley stared back at him with her mouth open and shook her head dumbly. Frank reached for the restroom door.

"She has a razor blade, Mr. Turner," said Valerie Buen.

"I know. Go find Ms. Weidman."

Valerie ran off.

Frank turned to the others. "Everybody go back to class."

Brittany clutched her phone. "We have to film it."

"You're not filming anything. Go back to your class."

Nobody moved. Frank waved his hand at them disgustedly, pulled open the restroom door and stepped inside. Heads poked through the open door behind him.

"Out," he barked and the heads disappeared.

The restroom was filthy. Graffiti covered the walls. Toilet paper and paper towels littered the floor and sinks. Dirty, blackened rain water dripped from a leak in the ceiling into a gray plastic bucket on the floor. It stank like a sewer.

Ms. Hope stood in the middle of the room, an old fashioned straight razor in his hand. His wig was off, revealing a shock of graying hair, and the sleeves of his red dress were rolled up to his elbows. He saw Frank enter the restroom and stepped back in fright. "Stay back," he warned, and waved the razor blade for emphasis. "Don't come near me."

"Put the blade down," Frank said.

"No! If you come one step closer I'll slit my wrists."

"And what, bleed all over the bathroom floor? Is that how you want to die?"

Frank heard the door creak open behind him. He turned to see Brittany Parker, phone in hand. She frowned and said, "There's no blood."

"Get out," Frank yelled.

Brittany ducked back into the hallway. The door closed.

Frank turned back to Ms. Hope. "Do you see what you're doing? You've got half the school up in arms."

"They're supposed to call me Ms. Hope and they weren't doing it."

"And for that you want to kill yourself? Come on, man."

"Don't call me 'man'!"

Frank spread his hands wide and stepped back.

Ms. Hope's voice was shaky. "I can't take it anymore. I'm going to kill myself, right here, right now."

"Put the blade down and we'll talk."

"No!"

"Come on. I'm trying to help. Put the blade down and then you can tell me all your troubles."

"Stay back!"

"I'm staying back."

"I told you, I can't go on anymore, I just can't."

Frank pointed with his thumb at the door behind him. "You want me to leave? I'll leave and you can stay in here all alone and kill yourself."

Ms. Hope shouted, "No, don't leave me."

"Then put the blade down."

The teacher hesitated.

"Put the blade down now or I'm going out that door."

Ms. Hope set the razor gingerly on the closest sink.

"Perfect," Frank said. "Now we can talk."

Ms. Hope stared at the blade on the sink and wiped his eyes. "They were making fun of me again."

"It's high school; we all get made fun of. *I* get made fun of."

"That's different."

"It's not different. It's just kids being kids."

Ms. Hope turned to Frank. "You don't understand. I gave up everything – everything – to live like this. People have to accept it."

"Says who?"

"Says the law."

"You're going to use the law to force a bunch of high school kids into accepting something they don't want to accept?"

"I have rights!"

"So do they."

"But I'm a woman, they have to accept that!"

Frank took a breath and said, "Look, don't get mad at what I'm about to say, all right? But you're not a woman."

"I *am* a woman!"

"You're not a woman, Scott. You're a man. You were born a man and you'll always be a man."

"Don't say that!" Ms. Hope burst into tears and grasped the sides of his dress. "This is who I am! This is me!"

The door creaked opened. Frank spun around to see Shelley Johnson, face aghast, staring at both of them.

"Get out!" Frank yelled.

Shelley disappeared back into the hallway and the door closed.

Frank turned to Ms. Hope and saw him grab the razor blade off the sink. Frank rushed forward. He grabbed Ms. Hope by the wrist and the two of them wrestled across the room, bumping into sinks and stall doors. Frank shoved the teacher up against the wall between two sinks, one hand on Ms. Hope's wrist, pinning it against the wall, and the other hand on the teacher's throat.

"Drop the blade," he ordered.

Ms. Hope shrieked in anguish.

"Drop it!"

The blade fell to the floor with a clang.

"Now you listen to me," Frank said. Ms. Hope tried to slip out of his grasp, but Frank shoved him back up against the wall. "Listen! Listen to me! You want to kill yourself? Kill yourself. But there are loonies all over this school that actually care about your sorry ass. You say you don't like being made fun of, well nobody does. But this is high school. You're around a bunch of immature kids and ignorant adults. Understand? Life's a bitch for everyone."

"I'm a woman."

Frank slapped him.

Ms. Hope shrieked and cried, "I'm a woman!"

Frank slapped him again. "You're a man, understand? A *man*. Nothing you do or say is ever going to change that. You were born a man, and if you kill yourself you're going to die a man." He gave the teacher an extra hard shove against the wall.

Ms. Hope turned his head to the side and sobbed. Frank released him and said, "Stop being so damn selfish. Think about other people for a change. Go back to your wife, Scott. Go back to your kids."

"I can't."

"Why not?"

Ms. Hope sniffled. "They won't take me."

"How do you know? Tell them you're sorry. Tell them you made a mistake. I'll go with you."

"You will? You'll come with me?"

"Yes."

"You promise?"

"I promise. I'll even speak to them myself if you want. We'll get the whole thing straightened out."

Ms. Hope nodded feebly. "Okay," he said, "if you go with me."

Frank sighed and stepped back. He heard a girl's voice behind him say, "Why isn't she dead?" and he turned to see Brittany Parker, Shelley Johnson and a pack of girls huddled in the doorway with their phones out, filming.

Ms. Hope shrieked and covered his head. Frank's face flushed red with anger. He stooped down beside the bucket of dripping rain water, picked it up and hurled its contents at the girls. The water hit them like a tsunami. They screamed and shrieked and fell out the door and into the hallway where they collapsed in a heap on the floor.

Chapter 12

Police and paramedics arrived. They questioned Ms. Hope and took him to the hospital. The girls who were soaked with the bucket of dirty rainwater phoned their parents and their parents phoned the school.

Esther Feinberg was livid. She had planned to slip out of school early to get a manicure, but now those plans had to be cancelled. She ordered her assistant to field the phone calls from angry parents and called Frank into her office. "Your behavior was deplorable," she told him.

"I was trying to save a life," Frank said.

"That's no excuse for what you did."

"Would you rather have a dead body on the bathroom floor?"

"I'd rather you not work here at all," Feinberg said, "and if you think I'm going to let you remain employed at this school after this latest stunt of yours, you're sadly mistaken."

"You're forgetting one thing."

"What's that?"

"You can't fire me, I'm gay."

Esther Feinberg slammed her fist on her desk.

Ryan was surprised to find Lucy waiting for him by his locker when the final bell rang. She leaned against the locker next to his, held her books tight against her chest with both arms, and said, "I wasn't sure you were here, I didn't see you in sociology class. I want to thank you for pulling that girl off me in the cafeteria."

"Are you okay?" Ryan asked, and yanked his locker door open.

Lucy frowned. "I have a knot on my head where she hit me." She touched the spot gingerly. "It hurts. I don't even know that girl. She had no reason to hit me."

Ryan lowered his voice and said, "You're white, that's her reason."

"That's messed up."

"Happens all the time."

"Will you walk with me," she said. "I'm scared to walk home alone now."

"Yeah, hold on."

Students rushed past them, hurrying to get out of the building. Ryan stowed his books in his locker and slammed the locker door shut. The sound reverberated down the hall. He looked both ways up and down the hall to make sure no one was watching them, and motioned for Lucy to follow him to the rear staircase. Their footsteps echoed down the empty stairwell. "That girl is still here too," Lucy said. "I saw her this morning."

"Are you surprised?"

"Yeah, I'm surprised. She should be expelled."

"That's not happening unless a teacher gets punched, and maybe not even then."

"If I hit a black girl I'd get expelled," Lucy said.

"You'd get arrested too. When it's the other way around, nothing happens."

Lucy cursed.

They reached the bottom of the stairwell. Ryan pushed open the door. Outside, a light drizzle was falling. Just inside the door was a knee-high stack of school newspapers. Ryan pulled two copies. He kept one for himself and handed the other to Lucy. They held the papers over their heads as makeshift umbrellas and stepped out into the rain.

"Where do you live?" Ryan asked her.

"Off La Brea."

They crossed the small courtyard at the rear of the school, stepped past the security guard in his enclosure, and walked down the sidewalk. The rain tapped a gentle patter atop the papers they held over their heads.

"I was going to get a tattoo this weekend," Lucy said. "But my head hurts so much I don't think I will."

Ryan scowled. "Well if that's the case, then it's good you got in a fight."

Lucy shot him a surprised look. "Why?"

"Because tattoos are stupid. Do you have any already?"

"No."

"Good. Don't get one. Girls with tattoos look like cheap," he was about to say the word *whores*, but stopped himself. "They look cheap," he said. "God sent you a knock on the head to get your attention so you wouldn't get one."

Lucy laughed. "Are you serious?"

"Dead serious."

"No, you're not."

"Just don't get one, all right? I don't want you to look cheap."

She glanced at him quickly. "Maybe I won't."

"No 'maybe'," he said. "Don't."

They crossed the street. The rain stopped and they lowered the papers they were holding. They passed the diner where the black girl worked. Ryan thought of her and a pang of guilt swept over him. The feeling confused him. He didn't owe any allegiance to either girl, so why did he feel guilty? Then he worried that Lucy might guess what he was thinking and he spoke quickly to distract her. "Are you ready for diversity training?"

Lucy cursed.

"You have a mouth," he said.

"So?"

"So you shouldn't talk that way in front of me."

"Why not?"

"Because I'm innocent and pure."

91

Lucy laughed.

They crossed another street.

"This is it," Lucy said, and she waved to a large white apartment building. She stopped on the sidewalk and turned to face him. "Thanks for walking with me."

"Sure."

She studied his face for a moment and said, "We should hang out sometime."

Chapter 13

Ryan was standing in front of Lucy's building two nights later when she strode out the front door, dressed in cutoff shorts, a T-shirt, and a denim jacket. Ryan took one look and cringed.

"Do you have to dress like that?" he said.

"Like what?"

"That." He nodded at her bare legs.

Lucy laughed. "They're just shorts."

"Do you have something else you can wear?"

"Are you joking?"

"No, I'm serious. Can you change into something else?"

"I don't believe this."

"Just do it as a favor to me, will you?"

Lucy turned and walked back into her building. Ten minutes later she emerged in a pair of tight black jeans.

"That's even worse," Ryan said. "Don't you have something else? Like a dress or something?"

"You want me to wear a dress?"

"I want you to wear something modest, something that covers your knees."

"I don't believe this," Lucy said. She turned and stormed back into the building.

"But not tight," Ryan called after her.

Fifteen minutes passed. Lucy stepped out of the building wearing the same T-shirt and denim jacket, but with a long plaid skirt that hung below her knees. She was accompanied by a woman in her late thirties. The woman was the same height as Lucy, with the same blond hair and the same snub nose. Ryan guessed her to be Lucy's mother.

"Are you Ryan?" the woman asked.

"Yes, it's nice to meet you, Mrs. Ford," Ryan said, and stepped forward to shake her hand.

Mrs. Ford smiled and said, "Lucy told me about you, but I had to see for myself."

"See what?"

"The kind of boy who would ask my daughter to dress modestly for a date."

Ryan stiffened. He thought he and Lucy were merely friends hanging out, but then he realized that Mrs. Ford would not have used the word *date* unless Lucy herself had used it in describing him to her mother.

"Anyway, I think it's wonderful," Mrs. Ford said. "You know, there's a word for that kind of behavior, a word that nobody uses anymore. Do you know what that word is?" She paused a moment and said, "Chivalry."

"We have to go, Mom," Lucy said. "We're late."

"Well, have a good time." To Ryan, she said, "That's my skirt she's wearing, by the way. It fits her perfect."

Ryan and Lucy started down the sidewalk. Ryan turned and glanced over his shoulder. Mrs. Ford was still there, watching them. She smiled and waved. Ryan waved back. He whispered to Lucy, "Did you have to tell your mom everything?"

Lucy whispered back, "She wanted to know why I kept coming back in and changing clothes. Anyway, it wouldn't have happened if you had let me wear my shorts."

"Why, so you can show off?"

"Maybe."

"Don't you know that pride is the beginning of all sin? You can go to hell if you want, but I'm not going."

"Don't say that, it's scary."

"Say what?"

"Hell."

"You told me you didn't believe in hell."

"You're making me believe in it."

At the corner they met Jason and Valerie Buen. Valerie was tall, almost as tall as Ryan. She was wearing flat shoes, but she still towered over Jason. With her arched eyebrows and braided hair, she reminded Ryan of exotic royalty. Jason stood next to her, grinning.

Valerie noticed Lucy's outfit and her eyes widened. "I love that skirt."

Lucy smiled wryly. "Thanks. It's my mom's." She nodded at Ryan "He made me wear it." She saw the confused look on Valerie's face and said, "I'll tell you later."

It was Hollywood's biggest night, the night of the annual movie awards and the girls wanted to watch the red carpet arrivals. They walked down the sidewalk towards the theater on Hollywood Boulevard where the ceremony was held.

Valerie said, "Crazy what happened in the cafeteria. And that teacher who tried to kill himself? Our school is crazy, huh?"

The street they wanted to cross was blocked. They went to another, but it too was blocked. Security was tight on every corner, police and private staff everywhere.

"We'll never get close enough to see," Valerie said.

"Don't worry," Ryan assured her. "I have a plan." They followed him down a side street, into an alley and then back towards Hollywood Boulevard.

"Where are we going?" Lucy asked.

"You'll see."

He led them to a gift shop on the ground floor of a three story building on Hollywood Boulevard. A bell above the door tinkled as they stepped inside. A teenage Latin boy with curly black hair watched them from behind the counter.

Ryan stepped to the counter and exchanged whispered words with the boy. The boy nodded and Ryan motioned for the others to follow him. He led them to the rear of the shop, through a stockroom in the back, and out the rear door to a small enclosed alleyway. Ryan spotted a blue milk crate and reached for it with his foot. The milk crate scraped against pavement as he positioned it under an old-fashioned metal fire escape. Ryan stood up on the crate and reached overhead for the fire escape ladder. It pulled down with a creak of metal hinges.

"Are you sure?" Jason said.

"It's all right. I've done it before. Follow me, but only one at a time."

He climbed the ladder to the fire escape and then climbed up the fire escape three stories to the roof of the building and waited.

Valerie came next, followed by Lucy and Jason. A waist-high brick wall surrounded the roof they were on. Ryan led them to the front of the building. Below them lay Hollywood Boulevard and a panoramic view of limousines lined up before a red carpet. An army of photographers were crowded behind the carpet, along with a crowd that shrieked whenever a celebrity emerged from a car and stepped forward. Lucy and Valerie gasped when they saw it.

"How did you know about this?" Lucy asked Ryan.

"The guy at the counter downstairs is a friend of mine. We come up here on the Fourth of July and shoot off bottle rockets and streamers. Just stay back a little," he warned. "Don't lean over the ledge. If the cops see you they'll think we're snipers." He saw Jason peering down at the street below and said, "Notice anything, Jason?"

"Everybody looks rich."

"What else?" Ryan said.

Jason shook his head.

"Where are all the homeless people we pass every day?"

"I don't see any of them."

"They kick 'em out every year to make the neighborhood look nice and clean for their awards. Tomorrow they'll be back, pissing all over the street."

"Look," Valerie pointed. "It's Emily Woodson."

Lucy and Jason turned quickly to see a lithe, blond-haired actress striding down the red carpet, cameras popping all around her.

Valerie pointed again. "And there's Lisa Wayne." She noticed Ryan holding back, standing behind them and said, "Don't you want to see, Ryan? They're famous."

"Famous for what? Turning out trash?"

Lucy smiled wryly. "Ryan says actresses are whores."

Valerie gave her a startled look.

"The men too," Ryan said.

Valerie turned to him. "Why do you say that?"

"Because they are. Look at the crap they make; everyone naked or half naked. They're causing people to sin."

"That's not like being a whore."

"Sure it is. They're selling sex, selling their bodies and their looks for money and attention. And guys all over the world are getting aroused by it and jerking off. How is that not being a whore?"

"But they're not having sex for money; they're not like literal whores."

"Actually, what they're doing is worse," Ryan said. "A literal whore only has sex with one person at a time, so their damage is limited." He nodded down at the red carpet below them. "These whores sell themselves to millions of people all at the same time. They cause millions of people to sin. And then young girls see that and imitate them, which causes even more sin. It's no different with the guys either. They're doing the same thing. They're all going to hell, the men and the women."

"Wow," Valerie said. "I never thought of it like that."

Jason nodded. "Ryan's deep."

"He's weird," Lucy said.

Ryan shrugged. "A genius is not without honor, except in his own home."

"Are you a genius?" Valerie asked him.

"In his own mind he is," Lucy said, and the others laughed.

"Do you watch movies?" Valerie asked Ryan.

"No."

"Television?"

Ryan shook his head.

"Nothing?"

"Why should I? Those people are all scum. They could use their money and their fame to help people. But they don't, because they don't care about anyone but themselves.

They can all rot in hell as far as I care. I'm not giving them a dime of my money. Bunch of half-wit Hollywood whores."

"I'm speechless," Valerie said.

Jason turned to her. "I told you Ryan was deep."

Valerie said quietly, "I don't want to go to hell."

"Ryan says everyone is going to hell," Lucy told her.

"*Almost* everyone," Ryan corrected her.

"Famous people too?" Valerie asked.

"Famous people most of all. I can't think of a single one right now that isn't going to hell."

"Hey look," Jason said. "It's Peter Wolfe."

The girls turned back to the street and looked.

Chapter 14

They remained atop the roof until darkness fell and the celebrities were all safely inside the theater. Then they climbed back down the fire escape to the alley below. Ryan thanked the boy behind the counter of the gift shop and shook hands with him.

The girls went to use the restroom at the nearby mall, where Lucy told Valerie how Ryan made her change clothes. "Stupid, isn't it?" she said.

"I don't know, I kind of like that he gets protective like that," Valerie responded, and Lucy felt a twinge of jealousy.

Ryan and Jason used the men's room and waited in the mall courtyard. When the girls returned, they walked around until Valerie suggested they get something to eat. Lucy recommended a diner close to her building, the diner where the black girl worked.

"No, not there," Ryan said. He suggested another location and led them to it. Sitting in a corner booth of the crowded restaurant, Valerie peppered Ryan with questions.

She paid more attention to him than she did to Jason, and again Lucy felt a pang of jealousy.

"Do you believe all that stuff you say in our sociology class," Valerie asked him, "about race and interracial dating and all that?"

"For the most part," Ryan told her.

Valerie said, "So if I'm hanging out with Jason, and he's white and I'm mixed, you think I should be whipped?"

Ryan shrugged. "That's for Jason to decide."

"Forget that," Valerie shrieked, and gave Jason a playful shove. Jason laughed and his face flamed red.

"Seriously, though," Valerie said. "What am I supposed to do? Mexicans call me soup or ketchup or chex mix, even though I'm not Chinese, I'm Filipino. And Filipinos call me flipsican or flipper, because I'm half Mexican. When I was little, I got picked on all the time by both sides, and I remember when I was seven years old, I was going to school in East L.A. and a teacher said, 'You must be adopted, you can't be brown like us with an Asian mother.' I'll never forget that. I can't remember anything else about being seven years old, I can't remember Christmas or my birthday even, but I remember that."

The others were silent. Finally, Ryan said, "That's one of the reasons why I don't like mixed dating."

"It's hard on the kids," Valerie said.

Ryan nodded in agreement. "It's hard on the kids and it destroys countries. It's destroying America right now."

"I'm kind of mad at my parents for that," Valerie said.

"That's one way of looking at," Ryan told her. "The other way is to figure that if they'd never hooked up you would have never been born."

"Yeah, I guess so. Maybe I should be grateful. I don't know. I'm all confused."

Ryan, feeling suddenly older, looked at her and Jason and said, "You need to think about what you're doing. You need to be careful."

Valerie's voice was somber. "Wow. Okay."

"We all need to be careful." Ryan said, and shot Lucy a look. She returned his gaze for a moment and then lowered her eyes.

Valerie said, "They get mad at you in class when you talk like that, huh? Especially the girls."

"They're idiots," Ryan said, and the others laughed. "I mean it," Ryan insisted. "The girls at our school are the stupidest, dumbest people I've ever met in my life."

"Tell me something I don't know," Valerie said.

Ryan pulled his phone from his pocket. He pretended to film himself and in a comic imitation of a girl's voice, he said, "Hey, guys, watch me shake it in my latest video. I'm wearing my cute little shorts and I'm dancing to my favorite song, and wait, what? How can this be? My video has no likes!"

Lucy, Valerie and Jason exploded in laughter.

Heads turned from across the restaurant.

Lucy said to Valerie, "I told you he's weird!"

103

Ryan lifted his hands in an innocent gesture. "Am I wrong? Tell me if I'm wrong."

"You're not wrong," Lucy said, and wiped tears from her eyes.

Valerie nodded. "That's like every girl at our school."

"It's their whole life," Ryan said, "the extent of their total existence. And the guys are even worse." He spoke in a low, guttural tone. "Yo, bro, check out this bitch dancin' in this video. You wanna get down with that, bro?" He changed his voice to a nagging mother: "Eugene, it's time for dinner." Then to an effeminate male voice: "I'll be there in a minute, Mom." And back to the low tone: "Bro, my mom's calling, I gotta go. Let's finish this video game."

His friends rolled with laughter and thumped the table with their hands.

More heads turned in the restaurant.

Ryan said, "All they do is watch porn, play video games and jerk off."

"That's our school, all right," Valerie said.

"It's every school in the country," Ryan told her. "We're a nation of retards. And everyone is going straight to hell."

Chapter 15

Ryan and Lucy walked west on Hollywood Boulevard. They had parted with Jason and Valerie after they left the restaurant and now they were alone for the first time all night.

Ryan noticed Lucy was walking close by his side, her arm brushing lightly against his, and a feeling of nervousness swept over his body. Soon they would arrive at her building and he would have to decide whether or not to kiss her. He had been thinking about it for the last hour and a half. Was she expecting it? Was she not expecting it? Would he make a fool of himself?

The fluttery feeling in the pit of his stomach was familiar and it reminded him of being nine-years-old and standing for the first time atop the high-diving board at the YMCA swimming pool, wanting to jump, but terrified of the height. Back then, he had his father cheering him on by the side of the pool and a lifeguard standing close by. Now he was all alone.

Lucy said, "I'm surprised you didn't want to see Emily Woodson. She's so pretty."

"You're better looking than she is," Ryan said, and immediately regretted it. He'd meant it truthfully, but he didn't want her to think he was smitten with her.

"No, I'm not," Lucy said.

Ryan paused for a moment and said, "I think you are."

She shot him a quick look and they walked on in silence. For the first time, he noticed how much colder it was than when they'd started out earlier in the evening. He said to her, "Are you cold?"

"I'm okay."

He felt his nervousness increasing with every step. His hands were shaking so he shoved them deep in his pockets. If this is how a date went, he never wanted to do it again. They crossed the street, walked another block and then they were in front of Lucy's building. She turned to face him, her green eyes glimmering in the moonlight, and said, "Well thanks."

He put a hand on her shoulder, leaned down and kissed her. Her lips felt soft and moist and instantly her arms were around him. The kiss lasted for an instant and for infinity. She broke the kiss and they hugged for a long moment, her head pressed against his chest. Then she pulled away gently and whispered, "Call me."

She squeezed his hand and he watched as she walked up the steps to the front of her building, unlocked and opened the door, and turned to wave at him. He waited for her to step inside and for the door to close behind her before he turned and walked slowly down the sidewalk. He guessed the time to be just after midnight.

It had been a long time since he was with a girl and the thrill of the kiss and the touch of her body against his was imprinted on his mind. He felt light on his feet. He didn't want the night to end.

Still, he wondered what he was getting into. The next time they went out, they would both expect to go further than a simple kiss and then what was he going to do? His desire for female companionship, his need to touch and to hold someone soft and nice, was overpowering. He would be tempted to sin and he knew from experience that he could only withstand temptation up to a point.

He spotted the diner where the black girl worked, its windows burning bright in the night sky, and felt drawn to it. He crossed the street to the beckoning neon lights, pulled open the front door and stepped inside. The room was packed with every table, booth and counter seat occupied. The girl wasn't there, only an older white woman. Ryan glanced toward the kitchen. The black cook wasn't there either. In his place was an older Hispanic male. Ryan turned and stepped back outside.

That was stupid, he told himself. He crossed the street. Ahead of him and walking his way down the sidewalk was a young Hispanic girl, showing a lot of skin in the cold night air. She had short black hair and was dressed in skimpy black shorts, a black tube top, and flip-flops on her feet. Ryan figured her to be drunk, a hooker, or both.

The girl said something over her shoulder to a squat Hispanic man trailing five yards behind her. The man said something back. Ryan revised his thinking. They now looked like a couple who had been arguing. They passed him and the man said to Ryan, "What are you looking at?"

"Nothing," Ryan said.

"I should kick your ass," the man said.

Ryan kept walking. He didn't want anything, especially a couple of lowlifes on the street, to spoil the mood he was in, not with the memory of Lucy's kiss still fresh on his mind.

He neared the bus stop on the corner and spotted a girl wrapped in a coat and huddled against the cold. The girl turned to register his presence and then turned away. A second later, she spun around and called to him. It was the black girl from the diner.

Ryan stepped closer. He noticed her shivering and said, "Are you okay?"

"I'm fine. I just get cold easy."

Ryan stopped in front of her. "What are you doing?"

"What does it look like?" she laughed. "I'm waiting for the bus. We were packed because of that stupid awards show so I had to work late. Now I missed my bus and I'm stuck here for an hour until the next one comes." She stomped her foot on the pavement. A thought occurred to her and she said, "Listen, can you walk with me to Sunset? There's an all-night drug store there and I want to get some cold medicine for my aunt. I didn't want to go alone, but if you're with me it should be all right."

"Sure," Ryan said.

They started off. Ryan glanced at her as they walked. Huddled inside her coat, only her face was visible, but he was surprised by how much prettier she looked now that they were alone. He felt a pang of guilt over his attraction to her. He'd just left Lucy and now he was with someone else. Another thought worried him. If romance between the races was so harmful, so destructive to society, then why was society constantly throwing temptation in his face? Why were the prettiest girls at his school all Hispanic and why were there so many of them? He glanced again at the girl and he remembered what he had forgotten to ask her in the past and said, "What's your name?"

"Agnes."

"Agnes?" Ryan raised his eyes in surprise. "You don't look like an Agnes."

"I know," she said with a trace of annoyance in her voice. "Everyone says that."

"I'm not saying it's a bad name, just that you don't look like an Agnes. Were you named after your mother?"

"No."

"An aunt?"

"No."

"Who then?"

"A saint. But you don't want to hear about that."

"Yeah, I do."

"Really?" She glanced at him and nodded. "That's right, you're Catholic. Me too. Okay, well Saint Agnes was a beautiful child and when she was thirteen, men wanted to marry her. She refused so they reported her to the governor as a Christian and she was sentenced to be taken to a brothel and raped. A gang of men dragged her naked through the streets to the brothel, but every man who tried to rape her there was struck blind. After that she was sentenced to death and beheaded. Because she didn't give in, she's known as the patron saint of chastity and purity."

"That's pretty intense," Ryan said.

"You bet."

They reached the all-night store and Ryan pulled the door open for her. "I have to get something too," he said. They went to an aisle stocked with school supplies and he pulled a box of crayons from the shelf. "For a kid in my building," he explained.

He followed her to the rear of the store and watched as she marched down the aisle, spotted the item she was looking for and plucked it off the shelf. "My aunt gets sick and this is the only thing that seems to help. I don't know if it's the medicine or her mind. Probably both."

"You live with her?"

"Yup. Since I moved here from Pittsburgh."

"What brought you here from Pittsburgh?"

"I came here to be a singer," she said. "I mean, I am a singer, but I came here to sing professionally. I had no idea what I was getting myself into."

"Tough business?"

"It's beyond that. When I first came out here a year ago I was completely naïve. I didn't know then what I know now."

"Which is what?"

"The music industry is satanic. Literally satanic. Movies and television too. All of them."

Ryan's eyes widened with surprise. "Seriously?"

"Oh yeah. All these girls," she rattled off the names of a dozen pop stars, "they all sold their souls to become famous. I mean literally sold their souls and made sacrifices to the devil for fame and fortune. Did you know that?"

Ryan shook his head.

"I didn't either until I came out here. When you see someone do this," she covered one eye with the palm of her hand, "or this," she made an 'okay' sign with her thumb and forefinger over one of her eyes, "it means they've sold their soul and they're going to hell."

"They all do that," Ryan said. "It's all over the internet."

"That's what I mean when I say the industry is satanic. But you know about rap music, right? How rap music got started?"

"On the street?"

"No," she said. "I mean, yeah, it started on the street. But that's not how it became popular. What happened was back

111

in the eighties, before most people had even heard of rap, the prison industry became privatized. That meant the more people in prison, the more money the prison owners made. So the prison people made a deal with the music people to promote rap music, knowing it would lead to more blacks going to prison. That's when rap music exploded. Before then, rap wasn't on television, it wasn't anywhere outside of the hood. But when the music industry started promoting it, suddenly rap was everywhere. And then what happened was exactly what they knew would happen: millions of black men began imitating the rap stars, acting like gangsters, and the prison population exploded. The prison people became filthy rich and the music people got a cut of all that money."

"That's unreal," Ryan said.

"It's totally true. It's like Pizza-Gate. It's real and it's earth-shattering, but nobody cares. Anyway, that's just the tip of the iceberg. I could tell you a lot more, but it would turn your hair white. I'm through with the industry."

"Can you go back?" Ryan said. "To Pittsburgh, I mean?"

Agnes lowered her eyes. "I'm afraid to."

"What are you afraid of?"

"Going home a failure."

"You're not a failure," Ryan told her. "If the music business is as bad as you say it is, then you're a success for leaving it."

Agnes turned to him with a look of surprise. "Wow, what a unique way of looking at it." She thought more of what

Ryan said and a broad smile crept over her face. "Thanks. I needed to hear that." She took hold of his sleeve and gave it playful tug. "Come on."

They started up the aisle. Ryan noticed she was walking close by his side, brushing against him, just like Lucy had. Again he felt a pang of guilt. They heard a shriek from the front of the store, followed by the sound of glass shattering. A girl cried, "Stop!" More glass shattered. Wild shouts filled the air. Ryan and Agnes quickened their pace. The floor beneath them trembled under a stampede of pounding feet. A middle-aged woman with a look of terror on her face rushed past them to the back of the store. They reached the front of the aisle. A massive crowd of black teenagers swarmed in front of them, grabbing merchandise from the shelves and running out the door. For every teen that exited the store, five more ran inside; an endless stream pouring in and out of the entrance, all of them whooping and hollering.

Behind the front counter, a white salesgirl cringed. A black boy leapt over the counter followed by two others with hammers in their hands. The salesgirl shrieked and covered the nearest cash register with her body. With one swift move, the first boy grabbed her by the hair, yanked her head back and punched her in the face. Blood spurted from the girl's nose. She screamed and fell to the floor. The other boys smashed the cash registers with their hammers.

Agnes reached for Ryan's arm and clutched it tightly. "Don't do anything," she whispered, "don't try to stop them."

113

Teenage girls smashed the glass cases in the cosmetics department. They filled shopping baskets with bottles of moisturizer, shampoo and deodorant. Teenage boys shattered the glass cases where the shaving products were located and stuffed their pockets with razors and blades.

Six teens surrounded an eight foot tall movie vending machine, pushing and pulling. It creaked and groaned as it tipped and landed with a shattering crack, spilling DVDs across the tile floor. Dark-skinned hands reached down and scooped up as many as they could.

A mob of teens surged towards Ryan and Agnes. Agnes pulled Ryan back and stood in front of him, hoping her skin color would prevent any attack. The teens flew past them to the liquor aisle. They grabbed liquor bottles off the shelves, stuffed them into the pockets and waistbands of their pants and ran crookedly to the door. Dropped bottles exploded as they hit the floor and sent splinters of glass flying.

A sprinting boy slipped on the spilled liquor and fell. His knee cracked hard on the tile floor, but he was up in an instant. He grabbed a case of beer from a display stacked six feet high and limped painfully to the door. Dozens of boys followed him. In seconds, the entire display was plucked clean.

Then, as sudden as the onslaught began, it ended. The last of the shrieking teens exited and the store cleared out. The salesgirl at the front register cringed on the floor behind the counter, whimpering like a wounded pup. Blood covered her face and blouse. The cash registers were empty. Every display rack in the store was overturned. The floor was covered with cracked merchandise, broken glass and puddles of alcohol. Everything was quiet.

Ryan and Agnes stood in stunned silence.

"I'm sorry you had to see that," she said quietly.

"I've seen it before."

She glanced at him, bowed her head and whispered, "I'm ashamed to be black right now."

Chapter 16

Frank studied the faces of his colleagues seated around him at the conference table. Every counselor and teacher at the school was present, save for Ms. Hope, who had been granted a leave of absence. Frank was struck by how ugly and unattractive they all were. Flaccid skin and dull eyes; everyone present looked at least ten years older than they really were. Frank knew that as people aged their faces took on the appearance of their thoughts, and he wondered if that was the case here.

Esther Feinberg sat stoically at the head of the table. She straightened her glasses, frowned down at the report on the table in front of her, and fingered the wooden gavel on the table next to the report. She said, "Well, our research data for the last five years is in and the results are conclusive. Teaching math at our school is racist."

Frank raised his hand. "Wait, hold on. How is teaching math racist?"

Feinberg peered at him. "The data proves it."

"How?"

Feinberg gestured to the report in front of her. "Over the last five years, in every mathematical category from algebra to geometry, our Asian students have consistently placed in the top one percent, followed by white students, Hispanic and Indian students, and then African American students who finished in last place. So that proves it. Teaching math is racist."

Heads nodded up and down the long table.

Frank said, "That doesn't prove anything."

Feinberg held up the report. "I just gave you the racial breakdowns. For the last five years, African American students have finished in last place in every mathematical category."

"So what?"

There were gasps up and down the table.

"*So what?*" Feinberg said.

"That has nothing to do with racism," Frank said. "Math isn't racist any more than history, geography, or music are racist."

Leonard Davis, a black male teacher in his sixties with a gray goatee and glasses said, "All of those subjects you mentioned are racist."

Frank turned to him. "How are they racist?"

"Those subjects were created by humans," Davis said. "Therefore, they come with human biases. White human biases."

"That's the most ridiculous thing I've ever heard," Frank said.

"Of course you don't understand it," Davis said. "That's part of your privilege." He pointed to Feinberg's report. "Are you disputing the results of the report Esther has?"

"I don't dispute the results at all, but it doesn't prove math or any other subject is racist."

"Then how do you explain the results? How do you explain Asian students finishing first and African-American students finishing last?"

"Gee, Leonard," Frank said with a trace of sarcasm in his voice. "I don't know. Maybe it means the Asian kids are smarter at math than the other kids."

There were more gasps around the table.

Davis sighed and shook his head.

Feinberg glared at Frank. "How dare you say that?"

"Say what? That Asian kids are smart at math? Your own report proves it."

"It does no such thing! It proves that teaching math is racist, that what it proves."

Frank held up his hand. "Hold on. Your report proves that Asian kids are good at math. That's all it proves. Maybe they study harder, or maybe their parents hire tutors, or maybe they're just naturally gifted at math, or maybe all of the above. Who knows? The one thing it doesn't prove is that racism has anything to do with teaching math. If the other kids are lagging behind maybe they should work harder."

Davis threw up his hands. "There you go again. 'Work harder, study harder.' Those are white ideologies."

"They're not white ideologies," Frank said. "They're universal ideologies. They're ideologies that work for every race." He glanced around the table for support. Teachers and counselors squirmed uncomfortably and lowered their eyes. The only teacher who met his gaze was Ms. Weidman, and she stared back at him with a look of defiance.

Davis leaned back in his chair. "Well, this certainly proves what I've always suspected. Racism runs in your family."

Frank turned to him. "What's that supposed to mean?"

"It means like uncle like nephew."

"You leave my nephew out of this. He's not relevant to the conversation."

"Oh, I think he is."

"Stick to the subject at hand," Frank said. He glanced around the table. "We're already graduating kids who can't read or write, and now we're talking about math being racist? These kids need math."

"They need diversity more than they need math," Davis said.

Frank turned to him. "What does that even mean: they need diversity more than they need math?"

"It means that unless and until they learn how to function in a multicultural, diverse society, two plus two equals four is not going to help them. We need to eliminate math and replace it with critical race theory for all grades, from freshman to senior. As teachers, as counselors, as administrators, we have that responsibility. We owe it to the children. We owe it to ourselves. We owe it to the world."

Ms. Weidman applauded. Others joined in. Frank said, "How do you expect young adults to function in the world without math?"

Feinberg said, "They can use the calculators on their phones."

"What if they want to be architects?" Frank said. "What if they want to be doctors? What if, God forbid, they want to be teachers? They can't possibly function in any of those fields without math." No one responded. Frank turned to Margi Holland, his fellow counselor. She lowered her eyes. He turned to Janet Bell, a fragile white woman with frizzy gray hair and lips painted pink. "Janet, this is your department they're talking about gutting. Don't you have anything to say?"

Janet Bell fidgeted with her necklace and spoke quietly, "Well, I'm not opposed. I'm willing to go along, you know, for the good of the students and the good of the school. Otherwise, you see, we're part of the problem."

"Part of what problem?"

Janet glanced nervously around the table. She leaned forward and whispered, "White racism."

Frank gave her a pitiful look. "They got you brainwashed too, huh?"

Feinberg slammed her hand down on the table. "That's enough." Frank started to speak, but Feinberg held up her hand and stopped him. "No, you've had your say. Now it's my turn. As educators we have an obligation to see that every child that passes through this school is equipped to function in modern society, both today and beyond. We also have an obligation to see that they are capable of embracing a multicultural world. Our students come here after eight years of primary school so they already have a basic understanding of math. Most of them, anyway."

Feinberg went on. "So I agree with Leonard, they need to learn the correct way to function in society more than they need algebra, geometry or math." She paused, studied the faces before her, and said, "Since we live in a democracy, we'll take a vote." She reached for her gavel and raised her other hand. "All those in favor of dropping math and replacing it with critical race theory, say, 'Aye.' "

Hands went up on both sides of the table, along with a chorus of "Ayes."

"Opposed?"

Frank raised his hand.

"The Ayes have it." Feinberg banged the gavel.

"This is insane," Frank said, "literally insane. Are we going to rename the school too? Joe Stalin High?"

"That's enough," Feinberg said.

"Karl Marx School for the Mathematically Challenged?"

"I said that's enough."

Ms. Weidman stood up. She cast a disdainful look at Frank and said to the others, "Come on, let's go celebrate."

"Sure," Frank said, "go celebrate. Celebrate the first civilization destroyed by the ignorance of its teachers."

Chapter 17

Ryan found Lucy waiting for him by his locker after school. "I'll walk home with you today," she said. "I want to see where you live."

"Are you going to serenade me?"

"Do what?"

"Stand outside my window and sing."

"No!" she laughed.

"Well, it's kind of a dump, so call or text me first if you want to come over. Don't just show up."

"I won't."

They left the school and walked slowly down Hollywood Boulevard. Lucy was in a talkative mood so Ryan let her talk. For the first time in days he felt a sense of peace. Trey was still in the hospital and Ryan was convinced that Marcus and his younger cousin Sam were not going to try anything.

They reached his street. Ryan stopped twenty yards out from his building and nodded to it. "This is it," he said. He waved to Talia, sitting on the steps in front of the building, but the child stood up and did not wave back. She watched, unsmiling, as Ryan and Lucy exchanged words and parted. She kept watching as Ryan walked to the building, unlocked the metal security gate and stepped through the entrance.

"Who's that lady?" Talia said, eyeing him.

"A friend of mine from school."

Talia stuck out her chin. "I don't like her."

"Why not?"

"She looks mean."

Ryan laughed and climbed the steps to where Talia waited. "She's okay," he said.

Talia looked up at him with pleading eyes. "Is she coming here again?"

"Maybe." He saw the disappointment in the little girl's face and said, "Guess what?" He kneeled in front of her, reached in the pocket of his jacket, and pulled out a box of crayons.

Talia's face lit up with surprise. "For me?"

Ryan nodded and handed her the crayons.

"Thank you, Ryan!" Talia clutched the box and her face turned suddenly serious. "Am I your favorite?"

"You'll always be my favorite," Ryan said.

The little girl grinned.

Chapter 18

Ryan and Lucy leaned back in their seats in the third row of the high school auditorium with stoic faces. Other white students occupied the seats around them. Standing on stage in front of them was an immensely obese black woman with a pointer in her hand. The woman had huge, ham-like arms, and she wore an assortment of different colored bracelets on her wrist. When she wielded the pointer the flab on the back of her arm jiggled and the bracelets rattled.

On a stand next to the woman was a large white poster board. Printed on the poster board in black letters were the words ALL WHITE PEOPLE ARE RACIST. Using the pointer, the woman tapped the word ALL.

"See this word? I want you to take a good look at this word. The word is 'all' and that's where I want to start. *All* white people are racist. Not some white people, not most white people, *all* white people. Now you might think that's not true. You might be saying to yourself right now, 'Who, me? I'm not racist.' Well, yes, you are. All white people are racist, including those who don't know it. *Especially* those who don't know it."

Lucy whispered to Ryan, "This is so gay."

Brittany Parker turned from her seat in the front row and shushed her.

The woman on stage went on. "Until white Americans are ready to admit, to confess, and to apologize to black Americans for centuries of racism, there will always be a great divide between us. So that's the first step: admit your racism. Step two is confess your racism. Confess and ask forgiveness. That's a requirement for all white people. Step three is apologize for your racism. Now an apology can be verbal or it can be monetary. By that I mean you can apologize by donating money to a black social justice organization, such as mine. You can donate money to a black person you know or even one you don't know. You can donate property, like your car or your house to a black person. Those are all ways that you, as white people, can apologize for your racism. And, of course, there are reparations, reparations for slavery, and we'll cover that."

The woman went on for ninety minutes. At the end of her talk she passed out papers to the white students sitting in the front row and said, "Pass them back. They're for you to sign and date." The students in the front row kept a paper for themselves and passed the others behind them.

A kid sitting in front of Ryan passed him one of the papers. Ryan looked at it and saw a series of numbered statements. The first statement read: *I, a white person, admit to being a racist and to practicing systematic racism.* The second statement read: *I, a white person, admit that I am responsible for the economic plight of Black Americans.* The third statement read: *I, a white person, admit to being guilty of racism towards Black People and I vow to make amends for my privileged and racist white behavior.* Ryan stopped reading and looked around him. Lucy, sitting next to him, looked at the paper in her hand and cursed under her breath. Other students looked confused or angry.

Ryan lifted his paper overhead and said, "I'm not signing this."

Students turned to look at him.

The black woman on stage tilted her head back. "You have to sign it."

"No, I don't," Ryan said.

The woman said, "You don't sign that paper, you have to take this training all over again. And you don't graduate."

"I want to show it to my parents before I sign it."

"Your parents aren't part of this training."

"Yeah, well, I still want to show it to them."

"Me too," said Lucy, followed by several other students.

The woman stepped forward. "Now listen, I'm talking to all of you: your parents aren't here. That paper is for *you* to sign and turn in. Not them."

Brittany Parker and Shelley Johnson signed their papers and offered them back to the woman. She took their papers and said to the other students, "Sign those papers and hand them back to me."

Ryan stood up and started for the exit. Lucy followed him. "Where are you going?" the woman demanded.

"Aren't we done?" Ryan said.

"No, we are not done. Not until you sign that paper."

"I told you, I'm not signing it."

"And I told you, you have to sign it."

"I'm not signing it until I show it to my mom."

"You want me to call your principal in here?"

All the students were watching now. Ryan shrugged. "Do whatever you want."

The woman threw her pointer down to the floor and stepped towards him. "Don't you roll your eyes at me. Don't you *dare* roll your eyes at me."

"I didn't."

"I saw you roll your eyes."

Lucy said, "He didn't roll his eyes."

The woman said to Lucy. "You stay out of this."

"But he didn't."

"I said stay out!"

"I didn't roll my eyes," Ryan explained. "I said, 'Do whatever you want,' and I went like this—" He shrugged his shoulders.

"You did it again!"

"I did not do it."

"I saw you do it," the woman shrieked.

Ryan laughed and said, "I'm not rolling my eyes."

"Oh, you think this is funny? This isn't funny at all and you ain't gonna be laughing when your white ass has to come back here next week and take this training all over again."

"Now look who's being racist."

The woman wagged her finger. "Nuh-uh. Don't you try that with me." She bent down with a huff, picked up the pointer from the floor, and swatted the poster board with it. "You see this? It says white people are racist." She aimed the pointer at Ryan. "That's you, you're racist. I can't be racist."

"Whatever you say."

"It's not whatever I say, it's the truth. You can't see the truth, because you've been a racist your whole life. You don't know what it's like to struggle; you don't know what it's like to be poor or what it's like to go hungry. You look like you've never missed a meal in your life."

"You look like you've never missed a meal either."

There were gasps all around the room.

Kids watched with their mouths open.

The woman stared back at Ryan, eyes wide and nostrils flaring.

Brittany Parker whispered, "Did you hear what he said?"

Shelley Johnson fanned herself with her hand, looking like she might faint.

Chapter 19

"Suspended again?" Ryan's mother looked up from her cluttered desk in the living room. "How can you be suspended again?"

Ryan handed her the paper he'd been told to sign. "They wanted me to sign this and I wouldn't do it."

His mother put on glasses and grimaced down at the paper in her hand. "What is this crap?"

"Diversity training."

"Diversity what?" She read the first three lines and said, "This is ridiculous."

"That's why I didn't sign it."

His mother sighed, removed her glasses and shook her head. "Ryan, sometimes in life you have to go along to get along."

"Go along with what?" He nodded at the paper in her hands. *"That?"*

"It's not the end of the world for you to sign something in order to stay out of trouble."

"You can sign it," Ryan said "I'll take it back to school tomorrow and maybe they'll take away my suspension."

She shoved the paper back at him. "I'm not signing this."

"Now you know how I feel."

"How long are you suspended for?"

"Three days."

"Three days?" She shook her head with disgust and turned back to her work on the desk.

Ryan studied her carefully. "I need to borrow your car tomorrow night."

She snapped her head up to look at him. "For what?"

"I have a date."

"A date with who?"

"Somebody from school."

His mother scoffed. "Your *date* is going to cancel when she finds out you're suspended."

"She doesn't care," Ryan said, "she's suspended too."

Ryan leaned forward in the driver's seat and gunned his mother's compact car up the steep winding streets of the Hollywood Hills. The night sky was pitch black, but the car's headlights cut a clear path. "You ever been up here before?" he asked Lucy, sitting next to him in the passenger seat.

She shook her head. "Nope."

"It's a drive, but it's worth it."

Lucy gazed out the window. "These houses must cost a million bucks."

"More than that," Ryan said. "A lot more."

"So is this where the rich live?"

"Some of them. A lot of creative people live up here. My uncle calls them hill dwellers."

Lucy smiled. "Hill dwellers. I like that."

They reached the top of the incline and Ryan pulled off onto the side of the road. Gravel popped under the car's tires. They opened the car doors and stepped out. There was no traffic, no ambient sound of the city below, only an eerie silence.

"It's so quiet," Lucy said.

"I know. That's the first thing I noticed too. Come on over here." Ryan motioned for her to follow him to a guardrail. Their footsteps crunched loudly over gravel. He stepped over the guardrail and extended his hand back to her. Lucy took his hand for balance and stepped carefully over the rail. Ryan led her to the edge of a cliff. Below them, as far as they could see, the lights of the city lay sprinkled across the landscape, sparkling like distant stars.

Lucy gasped at the view. "This is beautiful," she said, with a touch of awe in her voice.

"I thought you'd like it."

"I do. A lot. It's like a different world up here."

"That's why I come," Ryan told her. When I'm up here I feel like I'm on top of life, on top of everything. No problems, no troubles, just total peace."

"That's because there are no people here."

Ryan laughed. "That's part of it. The sad part is driving back down the hill and reentering the rat race."

"That's how angels must feel."

He looked at her funny. "Angels?"

"Yeah, you know. They're in Heaven where everything is perfect, but when they come down here to help us, they have to enter the earthly realm. Going from Heaven to earth has got to be a hundred times worse than for us going from here down the hill to Hollywood."

Ryan smiled and put his arm around her. She leaned into him and together they gazed in wonder at the city lights below them.

It was an hour before they returned to the car. Ryan slid a key into the ignition, but Lucy stopped him. "Don't," she said. "Let's just stay up here for a few minutes."

They sat back in the car seats and relaxed. Ryan turned to face her. He wondered if this was her invitation to fool around; to kiss and make out and maybe go further, but she was twisted away from him in the passenger seat, staring out her window.

"Are you okay?" he asked. He heard a light sniffle and said, "Lucy? Lucy, what's wrong?"

She shook her head and continued to stare out the window. Finally, she said, "Ryan, I'm a mess."

"So am I."

"Not like me."

"That's what you think." He heard another sniffle and said, "Are you sure you're okay?"

Lucy wiped her eyes and turned to face him. "Before I met you I was dating a guy, like last summer."

"Yeah, so?"

"So I got pregnant and I didn't know what to do."

Ryan waited for her to continue. When she didn't, he said, "So what happened? You had an abortion?"

"Three."

"Three? You had three abortions? How old are you, eighteen?"

She nodded. "It's like a ghost that haunts me. I think about it every day, every hour of every day, and I just want to die. Those little babies, they could have been mine. But I didn't know what to do."

"Did you tell your mom?"

Lucy shook her head. "No. It wouldn't have made a difference whether I did or not. She told me before, 'You better not get pregnant, and if you do, you better get an abortion.' I was so scared, Ryan, I didn't know what to do. What have I done?" She burst into tears.

He put his arm around her and she leaned into him, crying loudly. He felt her body heave against his with every sob; long moanful sobs, like an animal in agony.

Ryan drove his mother's car with one hand on the steering wheel. His other hand held Lucy's. The confined interior of the car felt suddenly claustrophobic. He wanted to help her, how could he not? But what could he do? And how could he possibly engage in any sort of romance with her now? Anything beyond a kiss was out of the question. A part of him wished he'd never gotten involved with her, but now it was too late. "Have you been to confession?" he asked her.

"No."

"You have to go."

"I don't know where ... there's a church in Hollywood."

"Don't go there. You need a priest that was ordained in the early sixties. Anyone ordained after that isn't valid. I know a guy, he's in his nineties; I can call him if you want. In the meantime, say an Act of Contrition and ask for forgiveness. Do that right away. Abortion is a serious sin, one of the worst. If something happens tonight and you die—"

She squeezed his hand tightly and they rode the rest of the way in silence. Ryan parked in front of her building and walked her to the door. He made no effort to kiss her. They hugged and Lucy smiled up at him, her tears dried, and stepped inside.

Ryan returned to the car and drove off. He did not see Lucy step back out of her building, or hear her call for him to stop. Lucy wavered for a moment to see if Ryan would turn back. When he didn't, she began walking in the direction of his building.

Ryan found himself breathing easier now that he was alone, but his mind was racing and he felt like a fool. He thought he was so wise telling Jason and Valerie they needed to be careful, but look at him: mixed up with a girl with three abortions. He felt bad for Lucy and he was still wildly attracted to her, but what could he do?

He drove past the diner where Agnes worked, and glanced ahead to the bus stop on the corner. He saw her standing there, hunched against the cold, and pulled the car over. He leaned over the passenger seat, rolled down the window, and called her name. She saw him and came to the side of the car by the open window.

"You stuck here again?" he said.

She nodded. "My relief was late so I had to work over."

"When's the next bus?"

"An hour, maybe longer."

"Hop in. I'll give you a ride."

She shook her head. "I can't."

"Why not? Where do you live?"

"In the Jungle, on Hillcrest." She saw his questioning face and said, ""It's not safe for you there. Even in a car like this it's not safe."

"I hate to see you freezing out here. Come over to my place, you can hang out for an hour."

Agnes hesitated.

"Come on," he said, and popped the door open for her. She held back for just a moment, then slid into the passenger seat and closed the door. Ryan pulled the car into traffic.

"Your car?" she said.

"My mom's."

"Will she mind me coming over this late?"

"She's not home." His mother was spending the night with Pierre again and the thought revolted him. Agnes noticed his change and said, "You okay?"

"Yeah, I'm fine. I was just thinking about something. You sure I can't give you a ride home?"

Agnes shook her head. "Not where I live. If they saw you there it would be dangerous."

"Because I'm white?" he asked.

"Because you're white."

He told her about the black teen who tried to sucker punch him at the subway station.

Agnes said, "A lot of black people hate white people, just hate them. But not everyone is like that."

"Why do they hate so much?"

"They think white people are hoarding everything for themselves and causing all their problems. They don't want to look in the mirror. Sometimes I wonder if they're all possessed." Ryan shot her a surprised look and she said, "I'm serious. Look at that mob we saw looting that store. Didn't they look possessed to you?"

"Actually, yeah, now that you mention it."

"They think they deserve all those things they stole, but they don't want to work for any of it. I don't want you to think all black people are like that, or even most black people, but a lot of them are. Like around forty percent."

"Wow."

"I'll tell you something else. I've had my tip jar stolen three times in the last year. All three times it was a black person that did it. One was a girl. And we were robbed at gunpoint once by a black guy. Thank God they caught him."

"I got this black kid in my sociology class," Ryan told her. "He says that black crime is caused by racism, and that looting is reparations."

"Oh, please. I know the type you're talking about. He's just repeating some Marxist dribble he heard from someone else and it makes him feel smart to talk that way. People like that are incapable of thinking for themselves."

"Would you like to live in a world without white people?" Ryan asked her.

"What? No. Where did you get that idea?"

"We talked about that in my sociology class."

Agnes sighed. "If white people disappeared tomorrow, black people would starve to death. I'm sorry, but it's true. Black people think, 'Oh, we'll get rid of all the white people and then everything will be ours.' But they don't realize that without white people everything would fall apart. Black people are just stupid. I don't mean to talk bad about my race like that, but they just are. You can manipulate them like that." She snapped her fingers.

Ryan parked on the street in front of his building and led her up to the second floor. "It's a mess," he warned her.

"Trust me," she said, "mine is worse."

He unlocked the door and they stepped inside. "Do me a favor," he said, "leave your shoes here by the door."

Agnes slipped off her shoes and surveyed the apartment. "So this is where you live," she said, and her eyes took in the cramped surroundings. She saw his cot in the hallway and stepped closer to it. "What's this?"

"What's what?"

"This thing in the hallway here."

"That's where I sleep."

"Here? In the hall?"

He nodded. "Pretty much. My mom has the bedroom and she uses the living room as her office."

"When I first met you, you said you were mad all the time. Now I know why."

Ryan laughed, but inside he felt a sense of shame. Agnes noticed and said, "I'm sorry. I shouldn't have said that." She saw the books on the table next to his cot and said, "Do you read a lot?"

"All the time."

"Me too. It's my only escape."

Ryan smiled wryly. "I used to read a lot of science fiction when I was kid. We were supposed to inherit a future filled with flying cars, mile-high skyscrapers, and rockets to the moon. Instead we have homeless people pissing all over the street, our cities are looted and burned, and we never even went to the moon."

Agnes laughed. "I know, right?"

She sat on his cot and he felt his heart quickening. He remembered bringing a girl home once when he was fourteen; a little red-haired girl from his school with braces on her teeth and dimples on her cheeks. They'd sat on the sofa, watched television and held hands. He'd even kissed her. But that was as far as they went. No girl had ever sat on his bed before.

Agnes noticed the card from Talia on Ryan's table and picked it up. "Who gave you this?"

"A kid in the building; lives on the first floor."

"The one you bought the crayons for?"

Ryan nodded. "She gave it to me when my dad died."

"It's beautiful," Agnes said. She placed the card back on the table and turned to him. "I'm sorry about your father. I can relate. Both of my parents are dead." She studied the titles of his books. One caught her eye and she pulled it from the pile. She read the title and her eyebrows arched high. "*White Power*? George Lincoln Rockwell? Are you serious?"

"That's a good book," he said.

"Really?" She opened it and leafed through the pages. "What's it about?"

"White power."

"Duh."

"No, seriously it's a good book. I mean, he uses a lot of racial slurs. Like really harsh, you wouldn't like it. And I don't agree with everything he says, but there's a lot of good stuff in there. He explains how the world really works and there's a great section in there on economics and how societies flourish when the economy is based on producing useful products instead of just making money, which is what we have now. He talks about the usual suspects too."

"Who are the usual suspects?"

"Read the book, you'll find out."

"Thanks, but my aunt would have a fit if I brought a book home called *White Power*. I do want to read it though. If you say it's good." She placed the book back on the table and scanned the other titles. Her eyes flashed and she plucked another book from the pile. "My favorite!"

"What?"

She held the book so he could see it. "*1984*! Remember, I told you."

"Right. When was the last time you read it?"

She flipped through the pages. "Gosh, probably two years ago. I need to read it again, but I lost my copy when I moved."

"Take it with you."

"Can I?"

"Sure." Ryan stepped closer. He pulled a light blue paperback book from the pile and gave it to her. "You've got to read this one. It's one of the greatest books ever written."

Agnes studied the cover. "*Our Lady of Fatima*, William Thomas Walsh."

"It's the story of Fatima," Ryan said. "You've heard about that, right?"

141

"I remember my grandmother telling me something about it when I was a little girl. Something about the sun."

"The Miracle of the Sun," Ryan said. "That book explains it all. Take it, I have an extra copy."

"Really?"

"You have to," Ryan insisted. "But promise you'll read it. It's that important."

"I promise." She smiled up at him and for the briefest of moments he found himself lost in her soft brown eyes.

"What?" she said.

Ryan shook his head. "Nothing." He felt her eyes watching him closely.

"You're blushing," she said.

"Am I?" He knew he was. He could feel his face flaming red.

"Yes," she laughed. "Only now it's worse. Your whole face is red. What are you thinking?"

"I don't know."

"You *know*," she said. "Don't lie to me."

Ryan hesitated. Agnes kept watching him, waiting. Finally, he said, "I was thinking of how pretty your eyes are."

"Oh." She sat up straight. "Oh," she repeated, her voice rising. "How old are you again?"

"Seventeen, I'll be eighteen in four days."

Ryan looked again at her eyes and again he drifted. He felt an overpowering urge to kiss her, to feel her lips on his. She sensed his thoughts and said softly, "Don't be shy."

He thought about Lucy and felt a wedge of guilt, and he thought about everything he'd read and everything his uncle Frank had preached to him about girls and the dangers of fooling around with girls, especially with ones that weren't white. But he didn't care. His physical attraction for the girl in front of him overpowered everything. Then he realized his mother was gone for the night and it was just him and Agnes alone in the apartment. If he kissed her, if he opened that door, it would almost surely lead to serious sin. It took every ounce of will power, but he forced himself to step back.

"I'm sorry," he said. "It's not that I don't want to – I do want to. But I just don't know if it would be right."

She nodded. "I understand. Totally. It's my fault, I'm tempting you."

"Definitely," he said.

Agnes laughed, but her laughter was tinged with sadness, and Ryan felt a pang of remorse for disappointing her.

She stood up and lifted the copy of *1984*. "Can I still borrow this?"

"Sure. Absolutely. Take both books."

She gave his sleeve a tug and said, "Give me a ride back to the bus stop."

They left the apartment and walked out the front door to the car. Neither of them saw Lucy, watching them in stunned silence from the sidewalk across the street.

Chapter 20

Ryan called Lucy the following morning, but she did not answer or return the message he left her. The same thing happened the next day. On the third day, he returned to school, his suspension over, but Lucy was absent from his sociology class. He glanced at her empty desk in the back of the classroom and wondered where she was.

His mind was still on Lucy when he walked home from school, past the panhandlers and the homeless tents on the sidewalk, turned onto his street and saw Talia sitting on the front steps of their building, waiting for him. He searched his memory for a joke to tell her, one he hadn't told her before, and he noticed an olive-skinned Hispanic man lurking in front of the security gate. Ryan paid the man no mind. He was still trying to come up with a joke for Talia.

The man appeared to walk off, then turned sharply and climbed quickly up and over the metal security gate and dropped down on the other side. He dashed up the front steps of the building, grabbed Talia, and carried her down the steps to the entrance of the security gate. A second later he was through the gate and running down the street with the screaming child in his arms.

Ryan watched, but it was like a dream, his mind not believing what his eyes actually saw. He stood paralyzed, almost in shock. Then his legs began to move, to run. "Drop the kid," he yelled. The man was forty yards ahead of him and pulling away, the weight of the child like nothing in his arms. "Drop the kid," Ryan yelled again. He hit his stride, arms pumping, and gained ground. Talia was screaming, drawing stares and dumbfounded looks from people on the street. Ryan was thirty yards back, then twenty.

The man turned off the sidewalk and ran into the street with Talia in his arms. A car slammed on its brakes and swerved to avoid hitting them. Ryan sprinted into the street after the man. A car horn blared, tires screeched against pavement. The hood of a car slammed into Ryan's legs and sent him stumbling, almost falling into the gutter. He righted himself and saw the man now thirty yards ahead. The side of Ryan's leg throbbed from the car's impact and he could feel a knot already forming, but he knew he couldn't stop. He shouted again at the man and kept running. The car that hit him sped off.

The man turned off the street and ran into an alley between two apartment buildings. Ryan shouted at the man and ran after him. The man glanced over his shoulder, saw Ryan sprinting towards him in the alley, and dropped Talia.

She hit the pavement, but was instantly on her feet. She ran screaming past Ryan, not even seeing him. Ryan caught a glimpse of the man's face. It was lopsided and deformed, with burn scars on the chin and neck. The man howled like a demon and rushed forward. He ploughed into Ryan and bowled him over. Ryan reached for the man's ankles to tackle him, but felt only a sharp kick in the wrist and heavy boots stomping over his shoulder.

He scrambled to his feet and ran after the man and out of the alley. His leg ached from the impact of the car and his spill in the alley and his breathing was coming in spasms. He saw the man running down the street in one direction and Talia running in the other, back towards their building. People on the street continued to stare.

Ryan hesitated, not knowing whether to pursue the man or to see if Talia was hurt. He saw Talia slip through the open security gate and up the front steps and into their building and he decided to check on her.

He limped back to the building, aware that gaping bystanders were stopped on the street and staring at him. They continued to stare as he stepped through the security gate of his building and climbed the front steps. The first floor hallway was dark. Ryan hobbled down the hall to Talia's apartment and knocked on the door. There was no answer, no sound from within. He knocked harder. A woman's voice whispered, "Go away."

He shouted breathlessly, "It's Ryan from upstairs."

The voice did not respond. He pounded hard on the door. "Open up, it's important."

The bolt inside turned. The door cracked open. Talia's mother, standing five feet tall, peered up at him through the crack in the door, the side of her face swollen from a purple bruise on her cheek, her eye half closed. "Go away," she said.

"Somebody tried to kidnap Talia," Ryan said.

"She told me."

"You have to call the police."

The woman pushed the door to close it. Ryan shoved it back open. The door swung six inches and snagged on a security chain.

"Go away!" the woman said.

"You have to call the police."

"We'll take care of it."

"Take care of it how?"

Behind the woman, Ryan heard Talia's sobs and the harsh whispers of a male voice. He tried to look over the woman's head into the apartment. The woman kicked at him and the door slammed closed. The bolt turned.

Ryan knocked, waited, and knocked again. But he knew she wouldn't open the door and he knew she wouldn't call the police. So he did.

The building became instantly quiet when the police arrived. Ryan told them what happened and gave them a description of the man. He stood by his door and listened as the officers went downstairs and knocked repeatedly on the door to Talia's apartment. He heard shouts and threats and the sound of the door being kicked in, and then more shouts and threats. When the voices quieted, he crept quietly down the stairs and peaked down the first floor hallway. He saw Talia's father, with his hands cuffed behind his back, being escorted down the hall by a pair of policemen. One of the men shouted at Ryan and he dashed back up the stairs to his own apartment and locked the door.

He knew that if he hadn't called the police, Talia's father would never have been arrested, but he reasoned he had no choice; that it was better for Talia's wife-beating father to go to jail, than for her would-be kidnapper to make a second attempt and succeed. Ryan knew if that happened, he would never be able to forgive himself. He waited for the ruckus downstairs to quiet down and then called Lucy. She did not answer.

He hung up without leaving a message and noticed his hands were shaking. He needed to calm down, to talk with someone about what happened. He went to the desk in the living room, pulled open the top drawer and fished out his mother's spare car keys. Then he hustled downstairs to his mother's car parked on the sidewalk in front of the building, and drove to the diner where Agnes worked.

The diner was almost empty when Ryan arrived. He went to his usual spot at the counter and slid into the seat. His hands were still shaking. His wrist was blue, with an ugly, swelling bruise where the man had kicked him, and he had bits of gravel in his hair from his fall in the alley.

Agnes saw him and her first words were, "Are you okay? You look white as a ghost."

"I'm fine," he said, and told her what happened.

Agnes gasped and covered her mouth. "Thank God you stopped him from taking that little girl."

"Yeah, but now her dad's in jail."

"So what? If he beats his wife, he deserves to be in jail. And I'm glad you're okay too." She held up a finger and said, "Wait here." She went into the kitchen and when she stepped out she had a huge grin on her face and a cupcake in her hands. A single lit candle poked from the cupcake's middle. She placed the cupcake before him with a flourish. "Ta-da. It's today, right? Your birthday?"

Ryan smiled. "Tomorrow."

"Well it'll be midnight in only a few hours, so happy birthday."

Ryan thanked her and blew out the candle.

"Wait," Agnes said, "did you make a wish?"

"I forgot."

"No, you can't do that!" She pulled a pack of matches from her pocket and relit the candle. "Now make a wish and then blow it out."

Ryan thought for a moment and said, "I wish that someday you'll go to Heaven and that you'll always be as beautiful as you are right now." He blew out the candle.

Agnes stepped back and covered her face with her hands. "I'm glad I'm black so you can't see me blushing."

Thomas came out of the kitchen and shook Ryan's hand. "You're eighteen? You're a man now."

Agnes said, "He's been a man for a long time."

"I'm twenty-two," Thomas said. "But I remember my eighteenth birthday. Had a fight with my girlfriend the day before so I went to the movies by myself."

"Awww," said Agnes.

Thomas shrugged. "Happens to the best of us."

"Thanks, both of you," Ryan said. "I really appreciate this."

Thomas shook Ryan's hand a second time and went back to the kitchen. Agnes turned to Ryan and her eyes widened. "I'm reading your book! The one about Fatima."

"Do you like it?"

"Are you kidding? I can't put it down. When I get home tonight I'm going to finish it. I don't care if I have to stay up all night long."

Chapter 21

Ryan arrived at school early on the morning of his birthday, worked out in the weight room, and then waited near the front entrance, hoping to spot Lucy when she arrived. It was four days since he last saw her and he began to seriously worry about her. He was still waiting when the first bell rang. Now his concern was mixed with anger; anger at her for not returning his calls. He threw up his hands and left his post.

Jason cornered him in the hall on the way to his locker and said, "Dude, you owe me."

"Owe you for what?"

"Valerie broke up with me. She said she thought about everything you said about life and dating and now she wants to be alone."

"Good for her."

"Good for *her*? What about me?"

"A little solitude never hurt anyone."

"*What?*"

Ryan left the uncomprehending boy standing alone and searched the other halls for Lucy. She was nowhere in sight. He began to wonder if she was even alive. His worrying intensified until after his first class when he spotted her shoving books into her locker.

"Hey," he said, "I've been trying to call you."

Lucy ignored him. She slammed the locker door shut and walked off.

Ryan followed her. "What's the matter with you?"

"I saw the girl, Ryan," she said.

"What girl?"

"What girl?" Lucy stopped walking and turned to face him. "The girl you were with after you dropped me off. The black girl."

Ryan flinched. "Her? She's just a friend. We hang out."

"Hang out?" Lucy said, her voice rising. "Like we hang out?"

"No, not like that. She's actually older. We talk about stuff."

"After midnight? In your apartment?"

"Yeah. She was waiting for a bus that night."

"How is she waiting for a bus in your apartment?"

"It was an hour until the next one so she came over to keep from freezing outside. Nothing happened. We're not like that."

"I don't believe you," Lucy said, and she turned and walked down the hall.

"There's nothing to be mad about," Ryan called after her, but Lucy ignored him. The bell rang and the hallway emptied. Ryan was late for his next class, but he didn't care. He stood staring after Lucy, trying to make sense of what just happened. He heard footsteps running furtively behind him and felt a sudden, piercing pain in his side, burning hot four inches in and then out again. The slicing pain caused a sharp intake of breath and he gagged, wanting to scream. He spun around and saw Trey holding a bloody knife.

Trey grunted and lunged at him with the blade. Ryan stumbled back, caught his balance, and ran down the hall. Blood poured from a wound in his side and seeped across his white T-shirt. Ahead of him was an open classroom door and he ran to it.

Inside the room, Leonard Davis stood before his class and stroked his gray goatee. On the blackboard behind him, written in bold white chalk, were the words AMERICA IS RACIST. Ryan staggered into the room with blood splattered across his shirt. Students saw him and shrieked. Trey entered behind Ryan, holding the bloody knife, and the shrieks turned into screams.

Shelley Johnson swooned and fainted in her seat. Brittany Parker leapt from her desk and ran out the door. Screaming students followed her. Ryan reeled towards Davis for help. The teacher dodged past Ryan and ran out the door with his students. Shelley Johnson, slumped unconscious in her seat, was the only student remaining.

Trey swung at Ryan with the knife. Ryan thumped against the blackboard and his body brushed across it. Blood from his side smeared over the words AMERICA IS RACIST. He stumbled to the center of the classroom, shoving desks and chairs at Trey, the metal-tipped legs of the school desks scraping across the tile floor. Trey chased Ryan around Shelley's inert body, feinting and jabbing with the knife, the only sound now coming from his grunts and the scuffle of his shoes against the floor. Ryan grabbed Shelley's history book from her desk and hurled it. The book hit Trey in the nose and he stumbled back and dropped to a knee. Before the boy could rise, Ryan stepped around Shelley's desk and swung a sharp kick into his face. It landed with an ugly, mushy pop. Blood spurted from the boy's nose and he collapsed.

Ryan took a couple of crazy steps back and plopped to a seated position on the floor. His side was ripped open and burning hot. Blood poured from the wound, but he could not stop it. It covered his shirt and ran over his hands. From the hall, he heard shouts and the sound of people running, but the classroom was quiet, Trey and Shelley both unconscious. It was then that Ryan lost consciousness.

Chapter 22

"How are you feeling?" The voice was Frank's. Ryan opened his eyes and stared up at the ceiling of the hospital room. Only a moment ago, he had been happily lost in a dream, talking with a young girl, a redhead, a girl he once knew; now he was awake and the dream was forever gone. Frank was sitting beside his hospital bed.

"You okay?" Frank said.

"How long have I been here?"

"Since yesterday."

Ryan tried to sit up, but the sharp, piercing pain in his side stopped him cold. Frank laid a hand on his shoulder and eased him back. "Relax, just relax. You lost a lot of blood."

An image of Trey with the bloody knife flashed across Ryan's mind and he said, "Where's Trey?"

Frank shifted uncomfortably in his bedside chair. "The good news is you broke his nose and you'll never see him in school again. He's expelled. Feinberg objected, but she had no choice. The police insisted on it. They arrested him too."

Ryan waited. When his uncle didn't elaborate, he said, "What's the bad news?"

"The DA dropped all the charges."

Ryan stared at his uncle in disbelief. Frank said, "Trey claims you called him a racial slur. So the district attorney, in her infinite wisdom, determined that he acted in self-defense and she let him walk. He's back on the street."

"What kind of crap is that?"

Frank shrugged. "I called her office six times, trying to make an appointment, but she won't return my calls."

"Who is this bitch?"

"Her name is Shaniqua Washington."

"I didn't say anything to Trey. He just came up from behind and knifed me. And even if I had, what difference does it make? It's attempted murder."

"I know, Ryan. But it's a new country we're living in and the traitors are occupying positions of power. What's wrong is right, and what's right is wrong. I'll try again, I'll keep trying."

"Get me out of here."

Frank shook his head. "The doctors want you here at least another day to make sure your stitches hold."

"I don't care. Get me out of here now."

"That's not a good idea, Ryan."

"I don't give a damn. I'm leaving. I'm leaving right now. If you want to help, fine. If not, I'll leave on my own."

Frank sighed. "It's your funeral."

"Are you gonna help or not?"

"I'll give you a ride, but then I have to go back to school."

"That'll work," Ryan said. He lifted the bed sheets, sat up gingerly, and swung his legs to the side. His feet touched the floor and a rush of blood caused his head to swoon.

"You okay?" Frank said.

Ryan nodded. "Just give me a minute." It took five minutes, but his head cleared. He found his pants, underwear and shoes in a small closet, but nothing else.

"Your shirt was covered in blood," his uncle said. He took off his jacket and handed it to Ryan. "Wear this."

Ryan removed his hospital gown and dressed slowly. His pants hung loosely on his hips and his uncle's jacket felt like a tent. He glanced in the mirror and was shocked at how thin his face looked.

Outside the hospital, he waited for his uncle to pull up in his car. He checked his phone, but Lucy hadn't called. He heard a girl's voice call his name and turned to see Mandy Patterson, a former classmate, striding towards him. She was a tall, rangy girl, with blue eyes and yellowish white hair. A year older, she had graduated last June. The familiar face made Ryan smile. Then he remembered the intense crush he had on her in his junior year and how she rebuffed him for being too young and his smile vanished.

She seemed to sense his thoughts and said, "You're not still mad at me, are you?"

"No," he lied, "it's good to see you."

She gestured to the hospital building. "My cousin had a baby."

Ryan wondered if he should tell her about his getting knifed and decided against it. He held his body perfectly still so she wouldn't notice him wince with pain and said, "What else are you up to?"

Mandy took a breath and stood taller. "I moved out. I'm on my own now and going to college."

"That's great," Ryan said. "Are you working?"

Mandy shook her head. "I'm taking a full schedule, plus extra classes so I can graduate early. I'm trying to graduate in three years."

Ryan remembered her as always being broke, always shopping for used clothes and bargain-basement deals. Even now she was wearing a denim jacket he remembered her bragging about two years ago because she'd found it in used clothes store for six dollars.

"How are you paying for it all?" he asked.

"I'm on social security."

"Are you okay?"

Mandy laughed. "I'm fine, but my dad died so I get social security every month until I finish college. I heard your dad passed. I'm sorry. I should have called you. Aren't you collecting social security?"

Ryan shook his head. "I don't know anything about it."

"Didn't your mom tell you? If your father died, you're eligible. I think it's until you're twenty-one or until you finish college. Anyway, that's what I did; everyone in my family. I have two sisters and a brother. They gave all of us papers to sign and now we're receiving money every month. Plus there was some insurance money. Each of us kids got a share."

Ryan's mind raced back to the days and weeks after his father died. He remembered no such papers.

"You should look into it," Mandy told him.

"I will."

She gave him her phone number and her email address. "Like I said, I'm on my own now. Call me sometime."

Now she wants me, Ryan thought. He forced himself to smile and said, "Sure."

Frank drove him home. Ryan half expected to see Talia waiting for him in front of the building, but she was nowhere in sight. He climbed the steps in front slowly and winced at the piercing pain in his side each time he raised his leg. He paused for a minute at the top of the steps to catch his breath and entered the building.

The entrance was dark. Ryan glanced down the long hall to Talia's apartment and saw the door was open. He started towards it, hoping to see her and willing to apologize, if necessary, for the part he played in her father's arrest. He heard men's voices coming from the apartment. He stepped to the open doorway and stopped. The apartment was empty. Two men, the landlord and a young Hispanic workman, surveyed a hole, the size of a fist, in the living room wall.

"Hey," Ryan said.

The two men turned to face him. "Hey, yourself," the landlord said. "Don't tell me you've got a problem."

"No, we're fine." Ryan nodded at the empty room. "Where's the family?"

"You tell me. They moved out two nights ago. Stiffed me on the rent."

Ryan stood stunned. "Are you serious?"

"No, I'm joking. They're hiding in the back bedroom."

The younger man laughed.

"They left?" Ryan said.

The landlord threw up his hands. "What did I just tell you? They moved out." He turned to the young Hispanic man, pointed to his own head with his index finger, and moved it in a circular motion. The younger man laughed again.

Ryan felt his cheeks flush hot. He wanted to punch both men in the face. Instead, he turned and limped down the hall. With every painful step came the slow realization that Talia was gone and he would probably never see her again. He heard the landlord's voice echo down the hallway, "If you see them, you let me know," and he felt his face flush hotter.

He climbed the stairs to the second floor and used his key to let himself into his apartment. The little Frenchman Pierre was sitting on the sofa in the living room and his mother stood at the sink, washing dishes. The smell of pork chops and spinach lingered in the air.

Pierre leapt to his feet and Ryan's mother turned to him with a look of shock on her face. "Who let you out of the hospital?" she said.

"I let myself out."

"You can't do that!"

"I just did."

"What did the doctor say?"

"I didn't talk to any damn doctors."

His mother stepped out of the kitchen. "Ryan, you can't do that."

"I'll be fine. I just need some rest."

"Ryan, we were going to visit you," Pierre said.

"He's right," said Ryan's mother. "We saved you some pork chops. We were going to bring some to you."

"What happened to you is terrible," Pierre said. "Absolutely terrible. What can I do to help?"

"Nothing."

"Anything, anything you want."

Ryan felt like saying, "Then get the hell out." Instead, he said, "I'm okay, thanks for asking."

His mother said, "Pierre means it, Ryan. Whatever you need, just let us know."

"I hear you had a date," Pierre said.

Ryan stiffened. The last person he wanted to know anything about his personal life was Pierre. He knew his mother had blabbed and he shot her an angry look, but she didn't notice.

"She must be a special girl," Pierre said. "I'd love to meet her. Perhaps we can all have dinner together."

"That's a wonderful idea," said Ryan's mother, and she turned to him. "What do you think?"

Ryan stepped closer, lowered his voice, and said, "Can I talk to you alone?"

"Why, what's wrong?"

"Nothing, I just want to talk to you about something."

"Okay," she said. "Pierre, will you excuse us?"

"Certainly. I'll wait in my car." To Ryan, he said, "Remember, Ryan, anything I can do for you, anything at all, just let me know."

Ryan's mother waited for Pierre to leave and for the door to close behind him, then said to Ryan, "Okay, Pierre's gone. What do you want to talk to me about?"

"Did we get money from Social Security when Dad died?"

His mother's face reddened. "Of course, we got money. I told you."

"You didn't tell me. What about me? Did I get money?"

His mother's face flushed a deeper red. "We're receiving money as a family."

"Every month?"

"Yes, I thought we went over this." She stepped back into the kitchen. Ryan followed her. "We didn't go over this at all," he said. "Were there papers to sign?"

"Yes, of course." She reached for a soapy plate and rinsed it under cold running water from the faucet.

"Were there papers for me to sign?"

The plate squirted out of his mother's hands and cracked into pieces in the sink. She spun around to face him. "I took care of everything, okay? What do you want?"

"I'm supposed to get money from Social Security every month, right? Until I turn twenty-one or finish college?"

"You're living in this house," his mother said. "Your money is going to the bills."

"Who signed my paper?"

"I signed it."

"You forged my name?"

"I told you, your money is going to the rent and the food. If you don't like it, you can move out."

"You forged my name?"

"It's not your money."

"It *is* my money. That money can pay the rent for me here, while you move in with Pierre. It can pay for me to go to college. It can pay for everything. You stole it from me."

"I didn't steal anything."

"You forged my name on a document! How is that not stealing? You're keeping all the money for yourself, just like you kept all the insurance money for yourself. I'm not getting anything."

She reached for the wall phone. "I'm calling the hospital. You're sick, you need to go back."

"Don't call anyone," Ryan shouted.

His mother paused, phone in hand.

"Just go," he shouted. "Go. Leave me alone."

She hung up the phone and stepped past him, picked up her purse from her desk and went out, slamming the door behind her.

Ryan pulled out his phone and called Lucy. Her voice message picked up. "It me," he said. "Call me, all right?"

His hands were trembling and the wound in his side throbbed with a biting pain. He moved gingerly to the hallway and lay back on his cot. He wanted to peel off his bandages and look at his wound, but he was afraid to. Afraid of what he might see; afraid that maybe he'd made a mistake by leaving the hospital. He placed a hand over his pounding heart and tried to slow his breathing. He closed his eyes.

He breathed deep, feeling his rage subside. Out of the tired cloud of his mind, he saw little Talia's face, her big bright eyes and her mass of black hair. He saw the playful look on her face when she wanted him to tell her a joke, and the somber look she held when she presented him with her homemade card after his father's death. He saw her sitting alone on the steps in front of the building, waiting for him to come home from school. He heard her calling his name, heard her laughing at his jokes. Before he could stop it, a sob broke in his throat. He covered his face with both hands and let himself cry. "I'll miss you, Talia," he said. "You're my favorite."

Chapter 23

Ryan felt small sitting on the counter stool at the diner. He hoped the jacket he was wearing would hide the ten pounds he'd lost from the stabbing and the way his clothes hung baggy over his frame. He hadn't told Agnes anything about the stabbing and she hadn't said anything or even seemed to notice anything about his appearance, but she was busy tending to customers and hadn't really given him a good look.

He watched her and a surge of loneliness swept over him. She looked as pretty as ever; her face, the shape of her body and the easy grace of her movements. Even her hands, the long, smooth fingers and the way she moved them, drew his attention, and he cursed himself for not kissing her when he had the chance. He had held out, in part, out of loyalty to Lucy, and also because he feared it would lead to serious sin. But now Lucy wanted nothing to do with him and his fear of sin was overpowered by his sense of desolation and loneliness and his attraction to the girl in front of him. If he

165

could just be with her, he thought, if he could just hold her in his arms and kiss her and know that she liked him too, everything would be all right in his world.

There was a lull in activity and she came over to see him. "Listen," he said, "do you want to come over when you get off work?"

Agnes smiled warmly. ""I'd like to, but I can't. This is actually my last night here."

Ryan stared back at her. "Seriously?"

Agnes nodded. "I'm leaving L.A. and I have you to thank for it.

"What do you mean?"

"I mean everything you said about how leaving the music industry is actually a success. And that book you gave me. The Fatima book. I finished it and it's changed my life. I just want to go to Heaven now. I don't care about anything else."

Ryan felt the color draining from his face. He didn't want her to know how devastating her news was. He said quickly, "Where are you going?"

"I'm going to stay with some old friends for a few weeks in Florida. And then from there either back to Pittsburgh or to live with my cousins in Mississippi." She wrote her phone number and email address on a slip of paper and handed it to him. "Here's my info. Promise me you'll stay in touch. Who knows? I might come back to visit."

Ryan smiled wryly. Customers called and she went to take their orders. Ryan watched her walk away, the gentle sway of her hips, and he knew that if he had kissed her when he could have, she wouldn't be leaving town now. He left the diner without saying goodbye.

Outside, alone in the cold night air, he felt a chill down to his bones and he realized the three people he most cared about in the world – Talia, Lucy, and Agnes - were now all gone. And in all three cases, it was his own actions that caused them to leave. Maybe it was for the best, he thought, at least with Lucy and Agnes. Maybe it was God's way of keeping him from doing something stupid and committing a serious sin.

He was fifteen yards down the sidewalk when he heard his name called. He turned to see Agnes standing outside the door of the diner with a worried look on her face. She called to him, "Where are you going?"

Before he could answer, she was running towards him. When she was five yards away, she slowed and opened her arms wide. "Come here."

Ryan took a step towards her and the next thing he knew, their arms were around each other. He hugged her tight and though the wound in his side ached fiercely, the touch of her arms and the softness of her body against his made his pain insignificant.

He heard her say, "If there's one thing in this city I'll miss, it's you." She raised her head and kissed his lips quickly and then again, longer, and then she broke the kiss and stepped away. "I have to go back inside."

Ryan watched her walk back to the diner, stop at the door and give him a quick wave, and then step inside. Once again, he was alone.

Chapter 24

Ryan awoke early the next morning. The silence in the apartment told him his mother was not home, that she had most likely spent the night with Pierre. She's going to hell too, Ryan thought.

He showered carefully, leaving his bandages on, still not daring to peak at his wound. He ate and dressed and was on his way out the door for a walk when his phone buzzed and he pulled it from his pocket. It was a number he didn't recognize so he let it ring through. Moments later he listened to the message that was left and heard the gushing voice of Valerie Buen, "Hey, Ryan, it's Valerie. Are you okay? I heard about what happened. Let me know if I can do anything for you. Call me. Bye."

He debated calling her and his phone rang again. He checked the number and saw that it was Lucy. He picked up.

"It's me," she said softly. "I'm out front."

"Out front where?"

"Your building."

Ryan met her on the sidewalk and led her up to his place. "It's kind of a dump," he said, just before opening the door. On the one hand, he felt embarrassed for her to see the squalid apartment where he lived. On the other hand, he didn't care. After all she'd put him through, if she thought less of him because of it, she could take a hike.

Lucy didn't seem to mind at all. They sat together on the small sofa in the living room and her only concern was his wellbeing. At her urging, he lifted his shirt, removed his bandages and showed her where he'd been stabbed. He was afraid to look himself, but Lucy wasn't. She leaned down and he felt her warm lips gently kiss the wound.

"I'm sorry about everything," she said.

"Don't worry about it."

A thought occurred to her and she said, "I talked to Valerie. She broke up with Jason."

"He told me."

"I think she likes you," she said, and shot him a quick look.

"I doubt it."

"I don't."

Ryan wondered if it was true and if Lucy was jealous. Maybe that's why she's here, he thought. Maybe it's the only reason she's here. He heard her say, "I want to do what you said. I want to go to confession."

"Seriously?"

Lucy nodded.

"Based," Ryan said. "When do you want to do it?"

"As soon as possible. You said you knew a priest."

Ryan nodded and pulled out his phone. He made the call, hung up, and said, "He's waiting for us."

"Now?" Lucy said, her eyes showing a sudden fear.

"No time like the present. You've been to confession before, you know what to do, right?"

"It's been a long time."

"Then tell him everything. Don't leave anything out."

"That might take an hour," she said, and Ryan laughed.

"Come on," Ryan said, "he's waiting."

They left the apartment. Outside, thunder boomed and a torrent of rain began to pour down. Lucy hesitated.

"How far is it?" she asked.

"Far."

"We'll get soaked."

Ryan smiled. He took her hand in his and together they walked down the sidewalk in the rain.

THANK YOU VERY MUCH for buying this book! If you enjoyed it, please share your thoughts by posting a review. People often make their book-reading decisions based on other people's reviews (I know I do), and your review of this book could be the deciding factor for someone who is thinking of reading it.

Whether you liked the book or not, I would love to hear from you. You can reach me at mikestone114@yahoo.com

If you enjoyed this book, you'll love my first novel: *A New America*.

A New America

On the most divisive day of the year, in the most racially-charged city in America, recently red-pilled movie producer John Duke is about to learn what political correctness really means: marching with the herd or losing everything, including his family.

5 Stars! "A well-written book of an America gone mad."

5 Stars! "More!! Great read!"

5 Stars! "An exciting well-written novel. The author uses no clichés, his descriptions are original, and as a whole the writing is very creative."

5 Stars! "A fast-paced exciting novel."

5 Stars! "Read it all in one sitting. Had to remind myself it's supposed to be fiction."

5 Stars! "I hope this book is read far and wide, because it is the truth."

5 Stars! "You would never see a book written like this in a mainstream publication."

5 Stars! "I read this book today and I loved it!"